"Melissa Fraterrigo's novel strikes with the unexpected force of a summer tornado. It's a marvel as gritty as the carnival at the edge of her fictional rural town of Ingleside, where characters worthy of a Flannery O'Connor story struggle and self-medicate to make sense of lives marked by loss, violence, and despair. Fraterrigo is as much a seer as her trompe l'oeil Fredonia the Great, who aches when she must reveal the truth. Fredonia tells her estranged daughter, 'Honey, I'll help you work toward any dream that you have. But this. This is not a dream. Laying hands is a job.' These characters yearn for one another, across time, even across death, and they take comfort in the past and in one another, however fragile their connections."

BONNIE JO CAMPBELL, National Book Award finalist
and author of *Mothers, Tell Your Daughters*

"Melissa Fraterrigo's people will brand an impression upon your soul. *Glory Days* is a heartbreaking cliff dive into a literary voice that stomps across the Midwest. She knows her land and its people, their struggles, conflicts, ways of survival and ruin, but most of all the roots to family, and wanting to escape that family. Her people are forever stained by their upbringing, memories, and consequences of choice. Melissa's stories are a powerful reminder of what it means to be human."

FRANK BILL, author of *Crimes in Southern Indiana*

"*Glory Days* is a tender and tragic portrayal of small-town life, filled with beautifully flawed characters whose voices are unforgettable. From this fascinating cast, we hear about the economic trials of farming, the realities of poverty, the solace of land. From calving season to an amusement park, this novel takes us on a journey that's told with generosity of spirit and a true tenderness for the land and people. A beautiful book."

LAURA PRITCHETT, author of *Stars Go Blue*

"Melissa Fraterrigo's *Glory Days* presents a world of ghosts and seers, the living and the dead, bound together in a small farming community at the crossroads of tradition and the most cavalier of progress. Spinning through a series of unforgettable characters, each lured by a sense of freedom, violence, or the need to belong, these stories surprise us, echo with significance, and draw together to paint a complicated portrait of a place about to be lost."

MICHELLE HOOVER, author of *The Quickening* and *Bottomland*

GLORY DAYS

Flyover Fiction

SERIES EDITOR: *Ron Hansen*

GLORY DAYS

MELISSA FRATERRIGO

University of Nebraska Press | Lincoln & London

Acknowledgments for previously published
material appear on page xii, which constitutes
an extension of the copyright page.

Epigraph: Excerpt of four lines from "Happiness"
from *The October Palace* by Jane Hirshfield.
© 1994 by Jane Hirshfield. Reprinted by
permission of HarperCollins Publishers.

Library of Congress Cataloging-in-Publication Data
Names: Fraterrigo, Melissa, author.
Title: Glory Days / Melissa Fraterrigo.
Description: Lincoln: University of
Nebraska Press, [2017] | Series: Flyover fiction
Identifiers: LCCN 2017011928
ISBN 9781496201324 (softcover: acid-free paper)
ISBN 9781496202994 (epub)
ISBN 9781496203007 (mobi)
ISBN 9781496203014 (pdf)
Subjects: LCSH: City and town life—Fiction. |
Interpersonal relations—Fiction.
Classification: LCC PS3606.R426 G58 2017 | DDC 813/.6—dc23
LC record available at https://lccn.loc.gov/2017011928

Designed and set in Janson Text by L. Auten.

For Estelle and Josephine

I think it was from the animals
that St. Francis learned
it is possible to cast yourself
on the earth's good mercy and live.

JANE HIRSHFIELD

Contents

Acknowledgments

This book is the result of the support and insight of many individuals.

Early readers improved these stories and encouraged me to keep going: Emily Guy Birken, Jo Honig, Nancy Patchen, and Casey Shipley, with a special thanks to Kathy Mayer, whose sighs made me think there was something in the world of Ingleside worth continuing.

Catherine Grossman, Alison Jester, and Barbara Shoup read the whole thing and asked hard questions. Brilliant editors then shaped these stories further: Kathleen Canavan, Jennifer Day, Jessy Goodman, Terry L. Kennedy, R. T. Smith, Valerie Vogrin, Dan Wickett, and the folks at New Rivers Press.

Fellow comrades Bonnie Jo Campbell, Alicia Conroy, Lawrence Coates, Wendell Mayo, Rachael Perry, Christine Sneed, Julianna Thibodeaux, and Adam Edward Watkins showed me that sometimes the best antidote is to keep going. Literary citizen Cathy Day inspires me to do more, while V.T., Barbara Kerkoff, and Dave Wieczorek always listened. Bob and Margaret Coon invited me onto their farm and answered my endless questions.

I am grateful to the Indiana Arts Commission, Purdue University Honors College, and the Purdue Creative Writing Program for the time and financial assistance to fine-tune these stories.

Sheryl Johnston remains not only an extraordinary publicist but also a truly kind one. Elizabeth Gratch infused this book with new life. Sara Springsteen, Rosemary Vestal, and the entire staff at University of Nebraska Press have approached this book with dedication and care, especially the amazing Alicia Christensen. Your faith in *Glory Days* means everything to me.

Thank you to my students past and present for having faith and bravely telling your own stories.

Sarah Anderson, Michelle Cooper, and Erica Klaw—your friendships make me a better person.

Thank you to my family, without whom none of this would be worthwhile. My parents, Carl and Judy Fraterrigo and Chuck and Betty Seymour, are a source of constant encouragement through their words and example. Chris and Jenny—you both keep me honest. Finally, thanks to Pete—your perspective always sheds light. I could not have done any of it without you.

I am grateful to all the magazines and their editors who first saw promise in many of the stories in this book: "Ghosts," *Shenandoah* 63, no. 2 (February–March 2013); "Ruin," *Sou'wester* 42, no. 1 (Fall 2013): 9–11; "Bait," *American Fiction: The Best Unpublished Stories by New and Emerging Writers*, edited by Bruce Pratt (Moorhead MN: New Rivers Press, 2015), 14:91–100; "Bastard," *storySouth* (Fall 2014); "Fredonia the Great" (as "Fredonia"), *Notre Dame Review* 38 (Summer–Fall 2014): 27–45; "Footer," "Printers Row Journal," *Chicago Tribune*, November 2, 2014; "Surrounded," *The Rumpus* (August 2015); "Teensy's Daughter," *storySouth* (Fall 2011).

GHOSTS

I DIDN'T BELIEVE HIM FOR THE LONGEST TIME. Three years since Mama's passing, and he continued to see her. Day before the sale I heard him scramble into his pants and flannel, laces crisscrossing, light still murky uncertain. I knew he'd caught sight of something from his bedroom window. I pulled on socks, and the back door swung wide. I followed him, imagined Mama's words in my ears, *Look after your father*, as if she'd known, as if somehow she'd known.

Outside Daddy's boots broke dirt clots, the little land we had left went on unplowed, just stubs of corn, old mud ruts now dry. He didn't want me to follow him. Tess! he called, my mother's name. How had he gotten so far? When I caught up to him, his face shined with sweat. I tugged his elbow. Let's go home, I told him, shivering with chill despite the wet heat. He took off. I heard emptiness rattle inside his shirt. He refused to eat; he said nothing tasted right. I looked up in the direction he ran, saw a woman in a gray gown and overcoat. She plodded firm with her back to us. Tess, he said to her. Please.

I didn't want what he claimed to be true. I had stood beneath the old oak where they set the stone with two engraved names. I thought I remembered crying.

I reached him again. He put a hand up to silence me. The sky peached, and the moon receded. We followed her across the colorless grass and into the trees. Briars caught on the length of her gown. Glare on the river, everything lifting with fire, a new day. We came up on her. He reached a hand out to her shoulder to turn her, and she looked at us—a stranger, eyes wild and unfocused. She shoved Daddy. No weight to hold him steady—and he flew, backside hitting a maple we sometimes tapped. The woman kept on, and Daddy looked dazed, egg-like lump rising on the back of his head—Tess? His face sheened white.

She's dead, I reminded him.

Luann, your mama's never gonna forgive me, he said, rubbing the bruise. Losing her people's land like this. We watched the woman descend into the river furrow, move along the dry bank. He told me that was no woman but a ghost, said ghosts were everywhere and they were nothing to fear. Your mama's the one I'm waiting for. Bound to come back to give me a piece of her mind. His shirt had opened wide at the neck, and I could see the rippled skin from his burns. It made me feel uneven. In response I petted my own neck, traced its smooth plane.

I tried to tell him there's no such thing as ghosts, but he gave me a hollow look like I had no real thoughts in my head. I was scared, and once we arrived home, I dove onto my bed, covered my head. Truth be told, if she were upset with anyone, it would be me. After a bit I tried to concentrate on summer sounds: peepers and gassy toads. I listened for her footsteps. Stiffened in my bed. Counted my breaths. Mama? It could have been ten minutes or an hour that passed. When I lifted the blankets, I blinked into darkness.

*

Mrs. Sparkman arrives early with two women from church. They set up the tables. Talk about the new priest, the upcoming pancake breakfast, the heat. They set out buckets of ice and jugs of sun tea. I bring stuff from inside the house and set it on the tables. Old clothes, the little jewelry she had. Dishes and kitchen things. A couple stained dolls. Daddy's in the barn with the men. As we work, the women ask me questions out the sides of their mouths. I am eight now. Do I like to swim? You must get lonely out here, no playmates your own age. They click their tongues. Wear looks of pity. I twirl with my arms up, white dress from Grandma swirling, curls scraping my shoulders; I stop when I start to get dizzy. They applaud. Say I am cute.

Come here, sweetie, one of them says. My left hand chews up my dress fabric. Come on now, she says, I won't bite. I obey, and she touches my hair. It feels like a sponge! Darleen, feel this. Another one comes by. Fingers my head. When they lift their hands, I slink away. Pretend I'm checking out the cookies set out on paper plates.

Gonna be trouble later. Nobody knows her people.

Hush. Girl's right there.

Mark my words. Adoption's not right.

More people arrive. Plastic bags hold purchases. The cash box fills. Everyone buys bits of us until only remnants are left— mismatched socks, an egg timer that doesn't work. I hold Daddy's hand when the auctioneer clears his throat and waves a hand in attention. The driest year Daddy can remember. July isn't even over and the trees have already dropped their leaves. Tassels on the corn are dry frittered things. Daddy had to give up the cows. There was nothing for pasture and nothing to pay for feed. The river smells of mud, decaying fish.

Daddy's not the only guy Papermill laid off; he's just the unluckiest, he says. The buckets of ice have turned to water by the time they are done. Some shake Daddy's hand or squeeze his shoulder. Take care now, they say. We sit on the steps and watch the train of cars leave land that has been in my mother's family for three generations—land the bank has sold. Dust whorls. We sweat. Vultures spoon the sky.

*

Two days he stays in bed sweating, ripe with fever. I sit beside him in a chair. Hold cool cloths to his forehead. Read aloud from books I own. Sadness seeps out of him. When he sleeps, he whimpers about the land or Mama, eyes half-lidded and dancing. Daddy, wake up. It's a dream. You are dreaming. I clap my hands around his. They are callused and feathered with hairs. He blinks awake, stares. I love you, Daddy, I tell him. I count to one hundred and back down. The fan whirs in its place on the dresser top, the faintest air moving.

I do what I imagine Mama doing. I wipe the counters with a mixture of vinegar and water and use an old fly swatter to beat dust from the curtains. I hang laundry on the line out back. Daddy is not whole and needs nutrition so I make a bowl of creamed wheat, stirring in the last bit of brown sugar. I sit at his bedside and try to rouse him. Time to eat, Daddy. Gotta keep up your strength. But he pays me no mind, and I know he is dreaming about her, that together he and Mama are making plans for more good times, like the ones he said they had before. I try to push the thought away but cannot forget that I am not of them. At what point will I be sold, given away?

That night I can't sleep. I am afraid of what may appear if I close my eyes. Instead, I wander the house and its empty rooms. I go to his bedroom and stand in the doorway. Stroke his arm to make him wake. Tess? he asks.

It's me, Luann. Your daughter.

What do you want? I don't say anything, and he scoots over. I situate myself right alongside him. The up and down of his chest and my chest. My fears evaporate. I promise I'll just close my eyes for a moment. Then it's morning, and I wake alone inside all that heat. The birds chirp, and the sheet is pushed back. My bedclothes are damp, and the bed is empty.

Daddy? I move through rooms vacant of furniture and rugs, and my feet make a dull echo. My heart bams away in all the silence. Outside crisp leaves sway.

I find him toeing the ledge of the barn's second floor, that open space that leads to nothing—morsels of hay, mouse droppings. Daddy, stay there, I say. I'm coming up. I speed up the rungs of the ladder and stand behind him, smell his sourness.

I'm not right, he says.

It's not you, it's times, I say and inch closer.

I was the one who planted that baby inside her, he says. His hair stands wild. I feel how close he is to the edge.

She says she misses me, he says, and she never used to say things like that. He drops his chin, and I grab his middle, yank him back until he collapses on top of me. The floor holds us. We both shake, and the dust in my nostrils burns.

The sun is all bared, and he sobs up against me, his back to my front. Air sputters out of him in choked bits. I hold him like this for some time, tight as I am able. I wish Mama would appear.

∗

They are building houses west of town on land that once belonged to the Doreghtys and Lamberts. RIVER'S CROSSING is what the sign says. We sit in the shadow of a hickory and eat apples dipped in peanut butter—food the church people leave on the step. You gotta eat something, I tell him, just like I imagine Mama saying.

I know, he says, palming an apple.

We sit so long waiting for Mama that my backside begins to tingle. She's different now, he says. Ingleside is different too, I think, only I don't say it. The deer are thin and sickly looking.

Smallmouth bass used to leap into a net extended from Red Arrow Bridge, but now they are pale scrawny things that barely ribbon the water. Daddy refuses to eat them. The bridge is near Papermill, and Daddy won't go near that side of town.

The bulldozers gnash the ground and drop black soil in mounds. The earth smells clean and looks rich, but the top layer blows away. Dust coats our eyes, lines the insides of our fingers and toes. The houses they are building have long peaked roofs and attached garages. Doors tall enough for giants. Tiny octagonal signs advertise security systems. The workmen hammer and drill, their backs bare and tanned.

We wait until the last crew drives off, and then I follow Daddy down to where the blacktop ends and the FOR SALE signs disappear. We head in a ways past drought-stricken trees to the crumbling brick of a hearth. I can see where the foundation once stood and cinderblocks are streaked black. The frame of a door and two windows stand beside that. He moves through the remainder of this house, and his boots catch on reams of honeysuckle. Daddy walks around as if he's trying to decide something. He stops and turns to me, speaks. They think you would be better off elsewhere, Luann. Living with someone else . . . His voice trails off. He won't look at me. He opens and closes his hands. Palms the skin below his shirt that still doesn't look right—never will be right. It's bumpy and disjointed from when he was burned as a boy.

I squint up at him. Do you think they're right? I ask.

He starts walking. A breeze curdles up from somewhere else and dries the sweat on my neck where my hair is pulled back. I feel like crying. When he keeps to his silence, I go and grab him by the pant loops. I want to stay with you, I say and watch the crazy panning of his eyes. He's here but not here. He lifts his arms a tad and does a half-spin, gestures, and I turn with him.

He talks. This used to be the kitchen, he says. Right here. My mother and father would sit here, and the twins sat on either side of mother. My brother Robert would be here. He strokes his neck again, the warpled skin, and I know he smells the smoke, feels everything crashing and ripping down around him. He runs a hand on the brick. Rubs it back and forth like the tracings we've made at school, only he's pressing down with his wrist and the skin's getting all scraped up and dotted with red.

As he talks pictures begin to appear in my mind, and I wonder if this is what it's like to see things, to be ghost haunted just like him. He points to the brush, to nothingness. I try to force the image of his dead family. I want to be more like him except in this way.

*

The first time Daddy saw a ghost he was just a boy out hunting pheasant with his younger brother and father. He held the gun in front of him, a hand on the stock and on the barrel. His brother Robert was a careful boy, a boy who wanted to please; he saw a flock of birds and aimed, but the birds scattered, and he fired, hitting Daddy. Hot heat poured from Daddy's arm, and he fell over at the sight of his blood spilling out onto the grass. Robert was unaware of his misplaced shot, and my daddy was too frightened yet to scream. There was a little flap of skin on his arm, white flash of bone beneath. And then a man slipped out from the trees, a tall man with skin as brown as deer hide. He snuck out, seemed to appear from the tall grass. The man passed a hand over Daddy's arm, and the blood dried up, went away altogether. The seam that had ripped open in his arm disappeared, and his skin was again whole. There were just a few stains on the grass to let him know it had occurred. By the time his brother found him splayed on the ground, the man had evaporated into the trees.

Daddy told his father he thought he saw Jesus. Son, he said, you must pray that happens in your lifetime.

*

Once the bank took down the sign from out front, the papers for the new owners filed, Mama came more frequently. I heard Daddy at the kitchen table with his checkbook and the security box late into the night, and then the chair would push back suddenly, and he'd up and leave. I learned to sleep lightly, to keep my sneakers tied. I never knew how long it would take or where he would go. Sometimes he wanted to be left alone—turned the handle as he closed the door soft and careful, and then I'd hear his boots thwapping the ground, and he'd be off.

I pumped my arms to keep up with him. I followed him across a rise into trees, then over a low wooden bridge, the river still beneath us. Tess! he cried, voice mournful. I did not see anything but his slight shape, the smell of the river's decay heavy and rich. He pointed out her form in the movement of some shrubs. I stared long and hard, and still she did not appear. But I'd watch with him, and the longer we sat, the more ghosts he saw: black people ragged and knobby kneed, faces clenched as they moved north. One time I stood there beside my father as he said a whole troop of them trudged in tattered clothes, faces worn. There were twenty, thirty of them. A baby cried, and a woman lifted the child to her breast. We stood there, and that time I did feel cool air moving. I had always known the route to the Underground Railroad cut right through these parts and Mama's people offered food, shelter. But I didn't see a thing.

The woman with the child held her out to Daddy, and he turned away, grabbed my shoulder and told me to start walking fast. It's one thing to see them, he said. Another thing altogether when they start seeing you.

And then nothing is as it seems. I find the skull of a squirrel, poke it with a stick, but then I see it whole, running along the underbrush, up a tree.

What is real, what is imagined?

Daddy tells me how the land was different before they adopted me, how he and Mama used to have a herd of more than seventy beef cattle. They used to make enough to attend the movies on Saturday nights, a nice ham and turkey at Christmastime.

We sit on the porch and watch the sun beat scabbed grasses that by now should have been corn, throwing shadows on our legs. He tells a story for every plot—points out where he first glimpsed my mother from behind a milking pail, the hill where he shot a buck; over there is where he says I took my first steps. You need to remember this, he says. I won't always be here.

Where are you going? I ask. He does not answer.

✳

Our last night, and the house is empty. I make Daddy drive me to Welmann's, where I use all our coupons on butter and sour cream, potatoes, eggs, ground beef. I make meatloaf and mashed potatoes pooling with gravy, buttered carrots in a glossy sheen. Now you eat, I say, a hand on my hip. My best Mama pose. I watch him touch the food on the chipped plate. The fork tines leave a ribbed impression and gravy floods from his potatoes. But he won't eat. His eyes have already started to pop from his face, excavate the bones on his cheeks. This worries me.

I finish my glass of milk, wipe my mouth, and stand. I have already fixed quarters to the bottoms of my shoes, tap in a little circle on the linoleum, and finish with my arms up, ta-da! He claps a few hands, says that is real nice, although he doesn't mean it. His eyes seem to brighten. Yes, yes, he says, nodding. Yes, she is.

Who you speaking to? I ask.

He chuckles, stubble on his beard flecked with white. It's your mama.

I don't see her.

She's right over there.

I walk in the direction he points, push my face in the corner of the room. Mama! It's Luann. You talk to me right now, and I stomp.

Don't take that tone with her, he says. She's still your mama.

Show yourself! I demand. I begin to think maybe Daddy really is crazy because there's no one here but us.

Later we unroll blankets on the living room floor, but it is too hot to even blink. Moths flick against the light outside the barn, and I wonder about the land. We aren't the only ones bought out by developers. Somehow I doze. Wake to buzzing, the click of the latch. Daddy?

I hear him shuffling away in his boots and slide on my sneakers. He hasn't gotten far. Once I fall into step behind him, he begins to run, and I follow. Daddy! Wait! I own a four-leaf clover pressed between sheets of waxed paper, the Bible from Mama's family. A lock of hair I cut from her when she was pregnant and napping and not yet dead. But I doubt any of this will work. Please stop!

He runs until he arrives downtown, a good two miles from our house. Both of us are sweaty and breathless when he slows in front of the ice cream parlor. He visors his hands around his eyes, presses his face into the glass. Sweat inks the back of his shirt and his armpits. She's fixing something, he says. I look through the window and see the counter with its striped stools, booths set with napkin dispensers. But I don't see anybody.

It's hot fudge, he says. Yow-wee. Extra cherries, Tess! You know it.

Behind us the sign for Bremeyer's department store glows red. Beside it are FOR SALE signs. The window of the realtor is papered with listings. All those panes of glass swallow his sound, send it right back at us. Hey! he says, brows drawn, mouth tightening. I tug his elbow. Let's go back, I say. I rush my mind to get him to turn around and head home. The animals are gone. The land has been sold. We should go back, I say.

Don't you want ice cream, Luann? He put a hand around my shoulder as he says this, looks right into my face as he speaks. Your mama is right there, and she's making us a treat. I look into the shop. I want to see something. Memories of my mother have evaporated into a kind of blurred uncertainty. Tess! He rattles the handle to the parlor. Let me in. His voice skims across empty storefronts, the two-story brick buildings. He grabs a cement ashtray parked next to a bench and heaves it up, veins in his neck popping.

Daddy, I say, don't do something you're going to regret. He elbows me away and in one movement swings the ashtray through the door; glass shatters, and a bell goes off, surprising us both.

He charges into the parlor, heels crunching and skidding on glass. Tess? His arm is bloody. The alarm won't quit.

Daddy, I say, let's go. He stands behind the counter now, palming the space. Lights flash red and blue, a siren. His blood pinks the smoothness.

She was right here. I saw her. He starts opening and closing the cabinets. Looking behind doors.

We've got to go. She's not here. And while I know he hasn't forgotten, know it pains him to hear it, I remind him she's in the ground on the hill.

The sheriff comes in then, hand on his holster. Hands up! he yells before seeing my daddy. Teensy? he says, his boots grind glass. What's all this about? and I feel the familiar pride as he steps forward, takes Daddy's hand. Sometimes they hunt together. Years ago Daddy helped deliver a calf for the sheriff's son and his wife.

Daddy shakes his head, offers a half-shrug. The sheriff presses paper napkins to the wound. It's hard times, is what Daddy says.

That it is, says the sheriff. Don't need to take it out on private property, you hear? He claps both hands on Daddy's shoulders and shakes them. You hear me? Gonna have to pay for this, he says. Daddy promises he will. The sheriff halts the alarm then directs us to leave. He offers us a ride in his car. I let myself in the backseat. Daddy's in front.

People are starting to talk, Teensy, he says, turning on the air conditioning. The first icy blast transforms my skin to plastic.

So let them talk.

I mean really talk. You've got to get hold of yourself or some-one's gonna do it for you. You got a daughter. He looks at me in the rearview mirror, forces a dopey smile. Think of Luann.

You think I don't know that. You think she's not on my mind constant? I'm so tired of everyone telling me what's right, what I can and cannot do. You people are killing me. His voice escalates. Let me out, he says, working the door.

What are you doing?

Daddy punches the door open and rolls out onto the grass. The car jerks to a stop. Insects dart in the beams from the car. The long road stretches before us. The sheriff swings his door ajar and sticks his head out. I could take you in, Teensy. You know that? Charge you on multiple counts.

Daddy ignores him, starts walking. The sheriff follows, the headlights catching shots of his back or legs as Daddy walks and we follow him home.

*

The next day is like any other. We roll up the blankets and chuck them in the back of the truck. The door rattles in its frame as he shuts it; the house is empty of us. Daddy drives to Grandma's house, empties boxes from the back of the truck and puts them in the basement. I don't answer him when he asks me if I'm ready, then turns the truck in the direction of Mrs. Sparkman's house. I don't believe him when he says Grandma can't care for me. Be honest, I think. She doesn't like me. Not of her kind.

He promises that he'll be back in a week. Tells me to mind my manners. He's going to Savoy for a few days to see about a job. He sets my bag just inside the door where Mrs. Sparkman tells him to leave it. Her house is warmer than outside and smells of stewed tomatoes. He gives me a hard hug. You be good now, he says.

As his truck pulls away, Mrs. Sparkman waves a handkerchief from the porch. Her bosom swells against the cabbage roses on her housedress. I refuse to look at him. I hear him turn his truck around in the grass. Dust lifts up. I try to ground my heels in the dirt, but I can't do it. I don't want to stay here. I am not going to be left behind.

Mrs. Sparkman calls my name, tells me to come back. I pump my arms until I'm running beside the truck. Daddy slouches over the wheel, won't look at me. He has the window down, the knob of an elbow out. I'm almost even with him when he gives it gas and shoots forward—and I choke on all that dust, bend over and spit, and when I stand up again, I see her a ways off in the crest of a hill—Mama's unmistakable step. Her nightdress is faded, but there is a rise in the belly, that almost-baby. I see her now and wave my arms—she's right here! Daddy, wait!

I believe you, I say, she's here! His truck keeps on, and dust eddies in its wake. Mom! I call, a name I rarely say. When she doesn't look up, I take off in her direction. She has shown herself to us both. But I will be the one to make her remain.

RUIN

NO ONE SEES HER SLIP OUT BACK wearing one of her daddy's shirts as a nightgown. They think Luann's in bed even though there's much to do. She pulls the wagon best she can, and her doll Tracey sits inside it. Luann maneuvers around a busted footstool, a plastic milk crate, and other things spit from the sky three days past. Tracey refuses to sit upright. She doesn't want to be here and keeps toppling over inside the wagon. The air is full of smoke, rot.

Luann finds a bodiless Barbie facedown in newspaper, yellow hair neon in the fading light. She tries to hide it from Tracey, but it's no use. The doll begins to tremble and demands that they return home. Luann picks her up, looks into her fear-globed plastic eyes, and pats her hard shoulder. It won't happen again, Luann says, uses a soothing voice. Repeats what her daddy has said: A storm like this only happens once a lifetime.

A tree fell on the train crossing, and now the bell rings constant, three days since the tornado struck. There are piles of boards, and the fence has collapsed, countless trees uprooted. Bump bump, Luann stops the wagon. There are dented cans of pineapple from Welmann's, a busted birdcage, a tan armchair with its price tag still affixed. Nothing they could afford, but now it's theirs. All of it. Anything Luann wants is for the taking.

Daylight has given way to that plumy color. Things underfoot snap and crackle. Tracey, never fond of the dark, pleads for them to turn back. We aren't supposed to be here, she says.

But Luann has noticed a furrow in the river grass, cardboard heaped in a sudden clearing. She sees a twisted hand. Thinks she hears a voice. Bends down, lifts the cardboard, and that first look of him sucks her breath away. His mouth is stuffed with grass, and his blue face is lifeless and still. Tracey buries her face in Luann's shoulder, begins to howl.

Let's go back, Tracey pleads through her unmoving mouth.

Be quiet, Luann says.

And then the boy speaks. It's okay, he says, coughs his words out like pebbles. Don't need to be afraid.

Leave him, Tracey says. There'll be trouble.

Hush now. Quiet. Luann repositions Tracey, pivots the doll's legs on her hip. Give me think, Luann says and knows these are her mama's words. Rubs her lips so they'll stop. She doesn't want to consider her mama now.

Help me, says the boy.

Tracey's the one who is confused, and the doll speaks up. But he's dead, she says. This boy is dead.

*

Moments before the tornado struck, the cows grazed in pasture. The horses were in the barn. Her daddy put halters on them and then opened their stalls and all the interior gates. He would have remained in the barn if Grandma had let him.

Luann, her grandma, and Daddy huddled in the root cellar just off the basement and listened to it roll down and hit. Screams pierced the ground, toppling everything. Luann's breath uneven, jittery. Jellied beets shivered in their jars. The cows lowed steady, and her daddy's face was stony. His hands broke open and shut. She knew if it were up to him, he'd lead as many of them as he could into the basement. But it's Grandma's house and Grandma's rules, and no matter how often he spoke of them getting their own place again, Luann knows now that will never happen.

It was not just the tops of houses but cars and trees, tractors, combines. It snatched up Red Arrow Bridge, its pieces scattered like toothpicks on Route 26. Even after it stopped, all that whupping rushed on. While her grandma cried, Luann waited for the cellar roof to crash, bury them. She never saw her grandma cry, and now she isn't sure she'll ever stop.

*

All day her daddy heaved loosened boards into a pile and then started a great fire in the pasture. Mr. Sparkman and a few other men came over a day after the tornado. They tied bandanas over their mouths and dragged the cows and horses, the ones that didn't make it, into one fly-swarmed heap. They found one of the horses ten feet up in a sycamore. Took two of them more than half an hour to get it down. Now the fire burns and snaps, black smoke rises. The stench bites her nostrils. She's supposed to stay away.

Stuff that's never had a smell, like her great-grandmother's Windsor chair, stinks. The dresser from her daddy's room on the second floor is without drawers and backside up on the front yard. The mattress from Luann's own bed is lodged in the window frame, bent like a hook. Walter Sparkman said they were lucky, said nearly twenty people died in Pruewood, where it first touched down. Ingleside was already flat, he said. Tornado just furthered that.

Church people brought food, blankets. Daddy didn't want to take it, but Grandma said they had no choice. Don't be stupid, she said, pulling on a donated Mickey Mouse sweatshirt despite the heat. Luann stood there, listened to them, traced the kitchen table with two fingers. Someone gave them a tent and blankets, and her grandma set it up in the living room on top of the rug. She refused to go outside. Darkness puddled her eyes. She cried and cried and said they were forsaken.

Crying won't help, Daddy said. We need to focus on rebuilding, cleaning up.

Grandma threw back her head, spoke the most words she'd said in days—You're crazy, Teensy. Bulldoze the whole thing. If you don't, I will.

Her grandma's been sad forever. She hates Ingleside despite being here so many years. Waited until Teensy went outside before speaking again, this time to Luann. What do you care? she said, jutting with her chin. This isn't your house. You don't like it, you go back to your own.

She waved her hand manically, that old person smell wafting off her as she shuffled to a cabinet of broken dishes, began to wipe the inside door with a rag. Winter grass pushed flat. Cornstalks tilled to the ground. Rotting smell. Train crossing bell in the distance.

Luann doesn't favor either of them right now, which is why she and Tracey snuck out to this land chalked with things. A hairbrush, books from the public library, a boy's bike curled up like a potato chip. Here's a desk miles from school. Everything suddenly spilled out on Grandma's property. It's like the whole world has been shaken and turned upside down. The handle on the wagon Luann pulls is crooked, but the wheels move just fine. Smoke rises, and the burning stench masks air.

He's not right, Tracey says about the boy. Maybe he's even diseased. And Luann, who has had things gathering in her for days, says, Enough! Takes Tracey with both hands and sets her firm in the wagon. Get me out of here, Tracey screams, pounds her feet.

I am the big person, Luann announces. You'll do what I say, or I'll throw you away like all this other junk.

Tracey quiets, and Luann leaves her, lifts the boy from his cluttered grave. She cradles him like a baby, although he says he's not. His legs dangle over her arm, much heavier than he looks. She clears the grass from his mouth and carries him to the river, stumbles beneath his weight. The water beats white and restless, churns with torn branches and garbage. A lawn chair does cartwheels farther downstream. Luann cups water and lifts it to his lips. Go on, she says. Drink. His hair fritters in the breeze, caught in the smell of ruin; she combs his hair with her fingers, soft and fine as rain. Something scurries across her foot.

I need to get home, he says, and his words seem to tilt, slant sideways. She holds him steady, and while she does so, he speaks. He tells her how the wind gushed in the apartment, blew the door off the pantry where they crouched, and snatched him from his mother's arms. A dizzy gray radiance ripped off his clothes, and he saw a car lifted hundreds of feet in the air. Glass and heavy moving things battered his body. There was the pop of power lines, and the slit of his rump cupped air. He tasted damp wool and old milk, whimpered hot and cold all at once; he heard screaming in the wind, everything swirled, grew thick. He tried to find his mother, but he felt only jagged things suspended. His bones buckled, cardboard draped him, and then everything became black.

Luann feels his tears, only they live deep, deeper than the space on his face, the eyes that remain open, glazed. It's over now, Luann whispers. How rough he's been worked. She pets his hair real nice. Water rushes past. She tells him to cry all he wants, wobbles as she rocks him. In the wagon Tracey waves her fist in the air. She pounds her feet on the hollow wood, yells for Luann to pick her up right this minute, to take her home goddamnit! And then she says what Luann already knows: the boy has begun to smell unkind.

Still, Luann swings him in her arms. Daubs his face clean with the hem of her daddy's shirt. She knows it does her no good to think of her own mama, the one in the ground, so Luann considers the one who birthed her, the one she knows nothing about. If Luann missed her hard enough, she wonders, might she return to claim her? She thinks of this as she rocks the boy. His loneliness, his stillness. Does anyone even know she's here?

I'm not going anywhere, she promises. He cries, and she holds him as the moon brightens up high. Smoke scrolls the distance, her daddy's work. And this, this holding on, hers.

BAIT

ONE OF THE CALVES CRIES A WATERY MOO THAT'S NOT RIGHT, and Luann knows they're finally here. From the bedside shade she sees them: seven to ten dogs lurk in pasture. They surround a calf, bend their heads, and creep in. A dog bares its slick gums and strikes the calf, takes her down, and then two more dogs pounce. The calf's last cry is muffled beneath cool animal weight. Rumps up, the dogs wag their tails as they work, nostrils blowing greedy slabs of air. The rest of the cows low insistent, chill smocked and slow moving, they circle the pasture unsure where to go. Teensy is awake. Luann hears him in the hall sleep-jogging; his hands sandpaper the walls. Goddamn, he mutters.

Don't know how to raise a daughter. Teensy tells her this all the time. And she doesn't know how to be one, she might say, if they were talking. But it's been four days now since he grounded her, and she isn't planning on speaking a word.

Hurry up, she thinks to the dogs. Kill or be killed.

Teensy fires the rifle, and the cows bumble-step, start their crazed mooing. Burst of another shot, and the back legs of one dog fold, but he quickly rises, rejoins the pack. Old wild dogs. They trot away. They take their time.

Luann scans the pasture for carcasses. Hopes they decimate the herd. She isn't going to be here much longer. Can't be baiting them every night. The cows form a semicircle around the fallen calf. Teensy walks out to the cows in his bedclothes and unlaced boots, flipped-out hair. He slips his arms beneath the calf and stumbles to right himself. The calf's black hair flutters against his arms, but the rest of her remains unmoving. Teensy carries it like a baby.

Luann drops the shade. Doesn't want to see anymore. Her blankets are warm, and she tosses them over her shoulders. Keeps hearing shots. Thinks maybe they are intended for her, for what she's done, bringing the dogs here. She presses a hand to her chest. Feels how the bullet would pierce marrow. Thinks of him bending over, lifting her, holding her like one of his calves.

*

Hours later, when the sun creeps from behind the edges of the shade, Teensy pounds her door, rattles the handle, and Luann wonders if he's figured it out. But then he says it's time to get up. Unbeknownst to him, she's been awake for hours. Luann finishes packing the duffel, stuffs it under the bed for later tonight. She pulls on a sweatshirt and then heads to the kitchen.

It's Friday, a school day, but Teensy's keeping her home to work the cows. Bowls of oatmeal steam on the table, her grandma's wiry hair pulled back into a button-sized knot. She asks Luann if she'd like more milk. Luann doesn't answer. If I'm not talking to him, I'm not talking to you either, she thinks. The old woman throws up her hands. "Fine. Do as you please," and she crosses herself. A few minutes later Luann hears the pop of the TV. The preacher sings a song of praise, and Grandma says hallelujah. "She must be praying for the cows," Teensy says while he eats standing over the counter. "Could have lost the whole herd last night. We got lucky, that's for sure."

Heat rises in Luann's face. Her hands moisten. She trains her eyes on her food, eats. Last few spoonfuls, and then Teensy drops his bowl into the sink. "I'll meet you outside," he says. "Hurry up. Joe Arbuckle'll be here in a minute." His face screws tight as he bends to lace his boots and then limps out the door.

He doesn't suspect a thing.

Luann wears Levi's and a hooded jacket, rubber boots that stop at her knees. The ruts have frozen, and she takes careful steps down the hill to the first sorting area. She knows how quickly accidents happen. Last fall a neighbor's horse threw Teensy when a bulldozer breaking up what had been the Ryan farm spooked it. Doctor said nothing was broken, told him to rest in bed, but Teensy was out there working later that day. He hadn't walked right since.

Teensy has backed his truck up beside the squeeze chute where they'll do the checks. He has on his straw hat even though the morning sun has gone limp. The wind bristles. A trail of blood spots the frozen grass, disappears. Luann wonders about the dogs, if any of them are dead. "Could have been worse," he says, without turning from the bed of the truck, where he takes caps off the bottles of parasite control. "The Moore's lost two calves last night. Thinking they went from our place to over there, sons of bitches." Teensy asks her to finish prepping the bottles while he sorts papers, fixes them to a clipboard. She does as she's told. Won't be here much longer. Clay is coming for her tonight.

All this grounding started last week when they met at Welmann's. Clay's got his own place in Pruewood, and that's where Luann is headed. Fifteen years old but short for her age, between the stacked pallets of paper goods and the hum of refrigerators in the grocery stock room, Luann let him work his blistered hands over her after she came up twelve dollars short at the register and he loaned her money. He shoved her bra up to her neck, dingy thing already stretched out like a pair of tube socks. She still doesn't know who saw her. Luann has the only brownish face in town. Of course someone ratted her out.

Luann is tired of fighting. Knew if she said even a handful of words Teensy would use them against her, turn what happened into an argument.

Clay is older. He has his own place. Luann is gonna go there for a little bit while things with Teensy blow over.

Mr. Arbuckle comes over the hill wearing a Monsanto T-shirt and coveralls. Not warmer than forty degrees, and his skin has gone pink like uncooked chicken. "Morning, neighbors," he says. Places his hands on the old barn boards that make the corral, lead into the chute. "How many we working?"

"Twenty." Teensy hands Luann the clipboard. "Let's do it."

"Where you want me?" Mr. Arbuckle asks.

"Head gate. Luann and I will bring them in." Teensy and Luann move behind the gate into the sorting area, where the female cows amble.

The yellow tag clipped to the cow's ear reads number 22. "Come on," Luann says, and her voice crackles with underuse.

"Got a frog in your throat?" Mr. Arbuckle asks, then shakes his head back and forth. He lets out a low whistle, stuffs a hand in his pants pocket. "You all grown up, Luann. I remember when you were an itty bitty thing." But she feels his gaze. It's true. Wasn't that long ago that her hips grew wide, her breasts came in, and even Teensy began to look away. Mr. Arbuckle's eyes trace her, and she shivers. Won't ever get used to those looks.

"Come on, sweetheart," Teensy says to the cow, holds open the gate while Luann uses a metal rod to poke her. The cow saunters into the corral, Teensy closes the gate, and Luann rams a two-by-four behind it to keep it from backtracking. "Let's hope Hartley's done his job." Hartley was their Angus bull. They put the female cows with Hartley throughout the season. If they weren't pregnant after three cycles, they sent them to the feedlot. Pregnancy checks were usually routine; only last fall, after the accident, Teensy was forced to reduce the herd to forty. Go any lower, and he'd take a loss, have to sell the whole lot.

Number 22 clears the corral, moves into the rusted chute. Her front end jiggles the scale, and Luann replaces the two-by-four behind it. Mr. Arbuckle croons. "Come here, darling." The cow takes two more steps, and Mr. Arbuckle pulls the handle and a gate comes down on either side of her head and neck, keeps her from moving side to side. She moos long and plaintive. "I know it," Teensy says. Luann dumps a bottle of pour-on over the cow's back and neck.

"Hear they arrested the Mattis boy?" asks Mr. Arbuckle. "Found him dealing drugs outside the elementary school. Selling weed to sixth-graders. Living in his daddy's camper, eating canned beans cold. This what we're turning to, Teensy? My father would take that boy and string him up by his ear."

"Yours and mine both. It's a new world."

Mr. Arbuckle snorts. "Don't like it. Can't even make a living farming. What can you do—sell drugs? That what we're supposed to do?"

A display clipped to one of the metal rails above the chute shows the cow's weight. Luann takes the clipboard from the truck bed and writes it down.

"What's her calving history?" Teensy asks.

Luann, who has the clipboard with all the papers in hand, pretends she doesn't hear him.

Teensy frowns, grabs the clipboard from her. "You gonna be this ornery, you can just go to school. I don't need this kind of help. Hear me? Your ears still work?" He yells close to her, and a thread of spittle smacks her jaw. He reads to Mr. Arbuckle from the paper. "Just as I thought. She calved last spring."

Luann considers it for a minute, going to school. Not to attend classes but to see her friends, get away from the cows and their soily smell. But she and Clay have already decided that if he gets off work early, he'll come straight to her house. Either way her dad's going to have a fit.

Teensy takes off his jacket, clips the arm's-length glove to the shoulder of his T-shirt, squirts lubricant up and down the hand and arm of the glove. He lifts the hinge and enters the squeeze chute near the back of the cow. The cow moos, and Teensy pats its flank. "Easy does it," he says. "That's right. Nice and easy." He grabs the cow's tail with his ungloved hand and holds it up. With the gloved hand he brings his fingers together like the closed mouth of some long-jawed animal; he closes his hand until the thumb tip and fingers are all connected. With his fingers forming a sixty-degree angle, he reaches up and pushes his arm into the rectum. The cow moans. She tries to wiggle her head, but her head and neck are secure in the gate. Once his arm is in, Mr. Arbuckle asks Teensy if he's found the cervix.

"I don't know."

"You want me to try?"

"Not yet."

Teensy's shoulder butts up against the cow. "If you still can't find the cervix," Mr. Arbuckle says, "you're too far in."

Teensy's face is pinched. "Can't feel anything," he says and pulls halfway out. Scoops out feces, then goes back in. He's inside the cow up to the top of his forearm.

"Check the lining. If she's pregnant, the lining'll be thick as a stack of pancakes."

"She's open," Teensy says and pulls out. Steps back and wipes his face with the ungloved arm. "Damn." Mr. Arbuckle releases the handle, and the head gate goes up. The scale rattles as the cow hurries off onto the frosted ground, moos. Teensy tugs on his hat. Limps a half-circle.

Mr. Arbuckle clears his throat, speaks. "I could call Chuck, get him up here this week maybe. Save you the cost of winter feed. We get the truck up here and sell them together, maybe we'll get a deal."

Here is where if Luann were a better daughter, kinder and more concerned with others, she would tell Teensy to keep the faith, just like she imagines her mother doing if she were still alive. Maybe reminding him of other times their backs were to the wall with a pile of bills and months without rain and they were forced to dip into the winter feed in July. But he doesn't look at her, and Luann doesn't have those kinds of words. Not for him. His hands ball into fists, then release. Blue-green veins pop from his skin.

She takes the clipboard back, makes a note in the records that number 22 isn't pregnant for the second season, according to the papers. The cow would probably be shipped off to the feedlot.

"Come on," says Mr. Arbuckle. "We just starting. Maybe you'll double your herd. You never know. Happened to me a few years back. Gotta be patient. Can't forget about the drought. That'll complicate things for sure."

Most people in town had sold their stock when the developers came, started buying up farms. Teensy, Mr. Arbuckle, and a few others were the only ones to hold on, although lately even Mr. Arbuckle had been saying he was getting too old for it. But it would take more than a check to get Teensy to cash in, which is why Luann had baited the dogs. She had opened two packages of bologna and placed them in the pasture the night before. Had been hoping for coyotes, but wild dogs worked too.

*

Luann couldn't recall the specifics of her mama's face. She could see her limp hair hanging at her shoulders, remembered her eyes from a photo, but she couldn't see how all the parts came together. Couldn't remember the touch of her hand or her voice singing some nursery song, but she could see her parents, the two of them working together, baling hay or tending to the cattle.

Instead, Luann remembered boys. Timmy Liszka. Seventh grade. Her first. Clothes draped him like a hanger. Someone passed a note in class, said he liked her. Luann with her dirt-clotted shoes and men's jeans. Eyes cast down, hair smoking her face. She let him take her out for ice cream after school. Told her a joke about their math teacher, and she nearly spurt milkshake out her nose.

Afterward he said they should cut through the woods. He took her hand, led her to a den of sickly cottonwoods, where he kissed her. Wet slurpy kisses. Saliva bridging their lips. Her hands quickly learned how to grab and hold on, how to squeeze and touch. And this type of learning comes easy to Luann. It doesn't earn her grades, but afterward there are signs she's doing something right. That steady look and hushed words. These boys make her feel special.

Now Teensy won't let her out after dark, so she has to make her plans for after school during that empty nothing time. She follows boys behind the trees to a place by the river where the rocks stack up and form an overhang; the edges are mossy, cool and wet smelling underneath. And there is a satisfaction that comes from this work.

When Luann was younger, she used to pray for blue eyes and her mother's fair complexion. Teensy's blondish hair. Even went through a time when she scrubbed with Ivory soap after a school girlfriend said she'd heard that's how you got rid of tanned skinned like Luann's. But no amount of scrubbing has helped.

What she wants is some quiet, some stillness in her head. How could she explain to Teensy that she knew—that she'd always known—that he blamed her in some way for her mother's death?

Lately all she can think about is that there is another place where she might fit in better. Maybe that place is Pruewood.

*

Number 30 is one of the youngest heifers in the herd. She and Hartley were spotted spending much of the summer together. The heifer is easily guided into the corral, but once she spots the squeeze chute, she tries to back up, starts mooing and wiggling her head. "I know, sister," Teensy says. Luann holds tight to the two-by-four, and Teensy pokes her forward.

"I'd be happy to check her, Teensy, no problemo," says Mr. Arbuckle.

"I've got it, Joe. Done this hundreds of times, and I'm a lot cheaper than the vet. Let's see what we have here," Teensy mumbles, guides his hand inside. He tilts his head toward the heifer, squints. "What the heck?" he asks, explains that the ovaries aren't swollen, the lining as thin as ever.

"I've had heifers like that," says Mr. Arbuckle. "Could still be pregnant, just real early. We'll check her next month. Could be a different story altogether then."

Luann swats number 57, an old compliant cow. She chews her cud as she enters the corral, doesn't stop walking until she steps onto the scale and the display blinks to life. Mr. Arbuckle clamps the head gate down around her neck, and Luann records the weight. "You want to do this one, Luann?" Teensy asks. He surprises her, this question. It comes out of nowhere. The cow flicks her ears back as if she's listening. "I'll walk you through it." Teensy's eyes are beady, intense. Angry. His gaze doesn't waver, and this menacing glare has become so familiar to her that it doesn't even register. They haven't gotten along for a while. Still, he's angry, and she doesn't know why.

Mr. Arbuckle chuckles. "You're crazy, Teensy. She's not interested. Heck, I'm only here 'cause we're friends and I'm expecting a beer or three later."

Teensy won't quit throwing dagger looks her way. She doesn't understand. "Well, I just figured you got all that time to toss perfectly good food to pasture that maybe it'd be time you earn your keep."

Mr. Arbuckle raises his eyebrows.

"What do you want from me?" she asks. "You spend your whole life catering to stinky animals." She crosses her arms and turns away from him. Luann tries to keep her shoulders straight, but everything feels rubbery, unright.

"How about some respect, for starters. Shacking up with every guy on two legs. You think I don't know?"

"Hold on, you two. Let's do some deep breathing." Mr. Arbuckle extends an arm, but he is still holding onto the head gate and can't reach either of them.

"If your mother were here, she would whip your ass so hard you wouldn't sit for weeks."

"Well, she's not, so you better do it." Luann's fury electrifies her. "I didn't take her from you. It wasn't my fault."

He blows air out his mouth. Forces a laugh. "This is crazy, know that? Just like you to turn it all around to you." He takes off the glove, throws it in a plastic bag hanging off the truck. "It's what you've wanted all along. Now you got your wish. Like Cinder-fucking-rella." He turns to Mr. Arbuckle, tells him to call Chuck, see how quick he could drive up and take the herd. "I'll bring a six-pack over later."

"Hold on there, buddy."

"Let her go," Teensy says to Mr. Arbuckle, gesturing to the cow in the chute. "We're done here." And then he starts up the hill toward the house, his whole body rocking with the effort.

Luann waits to feel some sort of satisfaction for the argument boiling to a head; instead, she thinks she might be sick. They didn't talk about her mom. And now it hung in the air—unspoken words had finally been said.

"You shouldn't talk to your dad that way," says Mr. Arbuckle. "Nice girl like you." He releases the lever, but number 57 remains in the squeeze chute. "You're a good girl, aren't you," he says to the cow. "Go on now, we're done." He swats her rump, and she lumbers out of the chute.

Luann watches Teensy. He is bow-legged, and his gaudy limp exaggerates the muscles in his back, and then, while watching him, it comes. She sees her mother in the hospital bed. A memory from long ago. Walls and sheets white, vinyl chair in the corner, but her mother's face a sad yellow, tube lifting up and down in a cylinder breathing for her. Her warm smell mixed with disinfectant. Her mother had lost several babies before and after they adopted Luann. That last time she refused to go to the hospital even though her eyes had gone wild, her face ballooned, hands and wrists doubled in size overnight. In the end Teensy explained that her little brother had died.

How come? Luann had asked.

'Cause he was no bigger than this, and he held up a fist.

Luann looks to the distance, way out toward the back of their land, imagines her mama in her overalls and flannel digging horse nettle from the pasture. Why did she have to keep trying to get pregnant despite what the doctors had said? And with this image comes the realization that theirs would not be the only farm to bankrupt. Every cornstalk in Ingleside would be yanked up and plowed over. Every empty barn reduced to a pile of board, replaced by sprawling homes with green lawns and fruit trees.

She understood that this life was going away with or without her.

Luann speaks to Mr. Arbuckle. "I'm bringing number 57 back around. You hold her, and I'll do the check." This time he laughs full and haughty, his belly rising up and down, exposing a thumb of stomach. "Girl, you don't know a thing about pregnancy checks."

"You'll walk me through it. Come on. I don't have all day." She catches up with number 57 in the far corner of the pen, starts poking its backside. "Come on, sweetie," she says. "Come on." Luann pokes and prods her up the hill with the metal rod. The cow flicks her tail, moves slowly.

"It's not like baking a cake," shouts Mr. Arbuckle from his place beside the squeeze chute.

"What's that?"

"I said—"

"This one calved in the spring," she says, "so she should be ready." Number 57 enters the corral, and Luann makes a smacking sound with her lips, draws the cow forward. Secures the two-by-four, and Mr. Arbuckle fixes the gate head. Luann grabs a glove from the box at the back of the truck. Clips it to her shoulder. Starts to add lubricant to the hand and arm of the glove.

"I could check her," says Mr. Arbuckle. "You hold the gate."

She ignores him. Enters the squeeze chute on the outside. The sun lightens behind the clouds, threatens to break through. She scratches the cow's ears, runs a hand over her neck and back before resting it on her rump. "Sweet mama," she says. The cow's eyes are blank and dark gelled. Its eyelashes are longer than most.

"Gonna have to push harder than anything," Mr. Arbuckle says. "Everything inside her is going to try and push you away."

Luann nods, draws her fingers together at a right angle just like Teensy, and then glides her hand inside the back end of the cow. She keeps her wrist straight, flexes her elbow. It's warm and tight. Muscles close around her forearm, and she doesn't know anything. Her fingers reach out, hope for something familiar. Keeps moving her arm up farther. "You'll feel the cervix," Mr. Arbuckle says. "It'll be a hard round shape. Now move just beyond that." She shifts her hand, and the cow moans, gives off a raspy bleat.

"Almost done," Luann says to it. She feels something—a ball of liquid?—and stops rooting. She looks up the hill, sees Teensy watching her. It's right here, she thinks, and tries to put it on her face for him—something real that is yet to come.

BASTARD

THE SUBDIVISION WAS BUILT ON LAND that once belonged to the Doreghtys, and as Footer peered into the house, gnats whizzed his head. Inside was a dark table with five chairs. Sweat slicked his armpits and neck, and a sour oniony smell rose from him. Footer knew he'd never belong in such a kitchen, his mom pouring juice into his glass or joking with his father about something that happened before Footer was even born. He tried to avoid thinking about her, but here it was all over again. His blood bubbled up into his face, and his hands grew tingly with rage. The anger seemed with him all the time now.

He moved over to a basement window and kicked it with his high-top. Just nicked the glass, but he was pissed thinking about her. It was a summer night, and heat surged from the ground. Locusts whisked the grasses. All those pretty little sounds she'd never hear. He kicked the window again. Glass shattered. This time he broke through.

Footer crouched inside the basement. His breath socked up in his chest, heart racing. He waited for footsteps or an alarm. But he only heard the tick of the water heater.

In the darkness he could see a plastic reindeer wearing a felt vest, a box full of framed photos, and half a dozen cases of soda pop. Who drinks this much pop, he wondered. Tried to focus. If he did it right, soon he'd have some money of his own. But just as quickly his thoughts returned to her. Didn't want to dwell on it, but he wondered what his mom would have thought of him breaking into someone's house.

Truth is he had no idea what she might think. He didn't have a single memory of her. She had never touched Footer. She never held him in her arms and rocked him or sang him a lullaby. She had never seen his face. Footer had spent his first few years of life with his grandparents in Chicago. Didn't remember much about them. They'd come to the States from Poland, worked at a bar owned by someone's uncle. How Footer ended up with his mother's brother, in Ingleside, he did not know.

If someone had tapped Footer's shoulder then, asked him what he was looking for, he would have shrugged. Footer's memory was like that. He would get hold of an idea, and then it would just abandon him. It was no surprise they'd put him in remedial classes at school, and one teacher had even hinted that he was slow. But the woman who taught English literature had complimented his imagination, the fantastic tales he could weave out of nothing. He'd always earned Bs in those classes without even trying. And then he started to do things like hide in the girls' bathroom or read a nudie magazine in the back of class when he was supposed to be working on geometry. He got a reputation for being odd, and he didn't mind it one bit. He liked shocking these girls. They were easy to scare.

What happened to his mother would not happen to Footer. The hand he had been dealt, his uncle might say. Most of the kids he went to school with had both a mom and a dad. Footer had an uncle who drank too much and when he did so shoved Footer against the wall, kicked him down the stairs, punched him until welts volcanoed his face. Come on! he'd say. Show me what you got. You some kind of sissy? Footer couldn't hit him. As much as he hated the man, he was the only one Footer seemed unable to hurt.

Footer finished high school and took a job cutting lawns and plowing snow, then for nearly a year worked the register at a gas station until the place closed. But it'd been months now, and he had spent the entire summer without work. He couldn't even get a job working construction in the amusement park.

Footer sidestepped stacks of newspapers and bins of clothes and headed up the stairs. His skin grew tacky inside the cool house, and for the first time all day the sweat that ringed his head dried. He scratched himself, and bits of skin flaked off.

At the top of the stairs was a glass case filled with porcelain figures and plates and another table with a piece of lace down the center. The walls were papered with some sort of scrolling design of greenish blue and pink, and even now at this hour, just the one light from the street outside, he could see what little sense these colors had existing alongside each other. Beyond this was another set of stairs and a chandelier that looked like cubes of strung ice.

In the room on the other side of the stairs, he discovered the TV hidden in an enormous cabinet. He palmed the remote and let his backside sink into fabric as soft as butter. Footer imagined himself sitting there as they came in—the police, the owners— because it was inevitable that he'd be caught. Footer Portman was not a lucky guy. In fact, he had the worst kind of luck, just like his mother. How else did she end up in the ground in some Chicago cemetery with what he assumed was the cheapest of graves, just her name, the date of her birth, the day she died.

He lifted his feet on the couch, propped a pillow beneath his head, and leaned back. It had been surprisingly easy. He'd over-heard some teenagers outside the liquor store where he bought his uncle's booze saying how the rich folks who lived here went away on vacation for months at a time and the house was just sitting there: a goldmine. He hitched a ride out to River's Cross-ing a day later. Knew if he waited any longer he was bound to forget. His mind was like a screen, and he never was sure what would stick.

The image of his mother did. Ania was her name. In the newspaper clipping he'd found in his uncle's dresser drawer, her hair was parted down the middle and real flat on the sides. It was the 1970s after all. His uncle was several years older than Footer's mother and was already out of the house by the time Ania was in junior high. Still, he must have known some things about her. Footer knew she had started nurses' training because it said so in the article—she had attended Rush University Medical Center, and he guessed she had been smart, into books and whatnot. So, how had it happened? Who was Footer's father, and how well did they know each other, and later, at the end, eight months pregnant, nursing school dropout, in the middle of one of the worst snowstorms of 1973 and only a man's army jacket to keep her warm—what had his mother been doing out that late at night?

A distant sound drew closer as tires moved thoughtfully on the newly paved road. Footer's heart quickened. His hands grew moist, his mouth dry, and the heat of the day again clamped down on him. He hustled upstairs, where he found a cul-de-sac of rooms and stepped inside the first one. Through closed blinds he could see a car with its headlights off. He opened one of the closet doors and slid inside, crouched down against a stack of shoeboxes as dress hems dribbled over his shoulders. He grew warm, and the air seemed to thicken. Car doors opened and closed in the driveway. And in this fear Footer had never felt closer to his mother.

He wondered if there had been an instant when it became clear to his mother that she was in trouble and that it would not end well. Here in the dark corner of the closet, he let himself imagine her. How Ania had been bundled in her dad's old army jacket, two scarves around her neck, a pom-pom hat. Someone at the school had encouraged her to take a leave of absence from her training. She was a single mother-to-be, but still she lingered around the hospital, took the bus there from her house, would bring an apple, a few crackers. Ania hadn't yet told her parents that she was no longer enrolled in classes. She parked herself on one of the benches outside the visitor's entrance and watched people come and go. Sometimes late in the day, when most of the nursing faculty had gone, she took her white cap out of her bag and pinned it on her head. She wanted someone to walk by and recognize her. Instead, everyone glanced at her face and then dropped their eyes to her belly. They turned away.

In the few sentences newspaper articles devoted to the woman who took his mother's life, Footer learned that Maria Torres had told her husband she was expecting. She had gained twenty-two pounds since the fall and wore a pillow beneath her dress. He pictured them assembling a crib in what had been the apartment's extra bedroom. Later they made a toast with plastic glasses of juice at the shower hosted by her cousins. She just needed the baby. And then one night she spotted a very pregnant-looking young woman walking three blocks from her apartment.

It had been snowing all day, but evening had come early, and the snowflakes that fell beneath the orange haze of the streetlights seemed larger, softer. Ania liked the way they ticked her face, and so she let her bus pass without boarding, decided to walk for a bit. What was the rush in going home? Her mother refused to talk to her, her father barked orders—telling her to get him a glass of milk or pick up the newspapers. She was gazing up at the huge flakes, feeling more content than she'd felt in weeks, shuffling through new piles of snow on the sidewalk, peering in the shop windows—relishing the glow from the blinking sign advertising an all-night restaurant.

That was as far as Footer got when he heard them in the house, running up the stairs, his heart beating so loud he was sure it would give him away. Everything he wore was soaked through with sweat. His mother had bled to death in a blanket of snow in the alley between a dry cleaners and an empty storefront, and Footer would die in the heat that had overtaken his body.

He heard drawers being opened and slammed, things turned over. And then it came to him that these were intruders and they were casing the place, exactly what they'd think Footer was doing if they found him inside the closet.

He squashed himself further against the wall, thought of his mother's face again, and it soothed him, this time a black-and-white photo he'd found in his uncle's room. It was a picture of the four of them—Footer's grandparents, his mother and uncle standing in front of a church. His grandparents were not smiling, noses straight as boards. It must have been his mother's first communion because she wore a little crown with a veil and stood there with folded hands. If he squinted, he could see where the softness in her face would disappear and the edges of her adult self would poke through. He shook his head, thinking of her. Why did she have to be so stupid?

His uncle stood off from the group, his head cocked to the right, just enough for Footer to understand that he didn't want to have his photo taken; he did not want to stand beside his parents and go to church or attend the celebratory dinner at an uncle's bar afterward. Later he wouldn't want to raise his sister's illegitimate son. He wouldn't want anything to do with him.

Someone was in the room where Footer hid. A tiny beam of light darted along the bottom of the closet door. The intruder threw open the drawers and dumped their contents on the floor. "Ain't finding shit," the voice muttered. If they were going to hurt him, Footer hoped it would be over fast. He didn't know how much longer he could stay folded up, sweating away, his heart ready to rocket out of him.

So, this is what it was like, he thought, seeing his mother's face, the one from the high school photo, only this time it was snowing great white flakes and she was moving down Ashland Avenue, past Woolworth's and an Italian bakery, the decision to let her bus go suddenly feeling like a bad choice. She had finished her thermos of water hours ago, back when she was outside the hospital, and now everything felt wrung with exhaustion. Her boots had worn a blister along the left side of her foot, so as she walked, she pushed this foot along, and if she were to turn around, she would see a heavy track in the snow from where she dragged it. She had enough fare for the bus, but she was some distance from the bus stop, and she could no longer feel her fingers or toes.

She hadn't cried when the doctor had told her she was pregnant and offered to talk with her boyfriend. She hadn't cried when George Portman had touched her middle and then pulled away his hand as if he'd been burned, and then he'd asked, "Why's your stomach so big?" And she'd said, "What do you think?" Already furious with herself, how foolish she had been.

The tears hadn't come during any of it, but now they made great warm streaks down her face, and she was miles from home, thirsty and tired. She had no one to blame but herself, she was thinking, wiping the snot on the back of her hand, when she noticed a woman in a navy peacoat and matching beret. A little thing, the woman was right in front of Ania. "There, there, dear, it's going to be okay. Maria will help you. I am here to help. The Lord God himself has sent me here to help you."

"Thank you," Ania said, her breath quick clouds. Maybe God *had* taken pity on her. The woman was so tiny, and her features were in miniature. Ania let the woman—Maria—rub her back.

This is what it would be like if I had a friend, Ania thought, and so she let Maria take her elbow. Maria said she lived around the corner and that they could go to her apartment and warm up. Ania was already thinking how nice it would be to take off the boots.

They turned into an alley, where the glow from the streetlight dimmed. Maria turned toward Ania and gave her a smile like what you might offer a new kitty. She opened her arms and pulled Ania into them, hugging her.

Maria is pretty and small, Ania thought. She is my new friend. Ania sank into the warmth of her friend's body until an abrupt chill moved in, gripping her. She took a step back and could see that Maria was no longer smiling. She had unzipped Ania's coat, which confused her. Had Maria wanted to see her clothes? "Esto es mio," Maria said, thrusting a fist forward into Ania's stomach. Ania stumbled and fell, all that soft snow feathering up around her. But on the ground the hurt seemed to spread, and that's when she saw Maria's hand and part of her arm deep inside her stomach. An ugly ache clamped down on Ania, ricocheted through her body. She pressed a now-wet mitten on the oozing wound and then tried to push Maria away. She thought the idea, but Maria, pretty and small Maria, seemed so much stronger. "*No!*" Ania cried. "Please stop," she sobbed. This woman was not her friend. "Please," she said. It was the only thing she could think to say.

Maria hesitated. "No te preocupes," she said. "I take good care," and then she offered that perfect bow smile and pushed Ania back into a pile of snow, only this time Ania could not lift herself. She watched Maria work inside her, saw the dull glint of the blade, and a great rollicking wave of agony contorted her. Ania vomited, but since she was lying down, only part of it left her; the rest slithered down the side of her face. Maria pushed aside part of her swollen belly and yanked and yanked. She could no longer keep her head erect, felt her flesh being turned and twisted. And then Footer felt himself rolled to the side and lifted, the white beam from the flashlight on his face, and all that sweat was met by dry air as they yanked him from the floor of the closet and shoved him hard and fast against the bedroom wall.

"Who's this asshole?" They didn't wait for a response. They cuffed him across the face, and Footer refrained from moving anything at all except for his eyes, which shot from the guy holding the flashlight to the one in a tank top and high-tops.

"How'd this fat fuck end up here?" The guy with the flashlight asked. The other one shook his head, didn't turn his gaze from Footer's. Finally, out the side of his mouth, he said, "Give us the dough."

This is where Footer had to laugh, a friendly chuckle breaking the static coolness of the house because he *had* wanted money, he'd initially been interested in finding cash, stuffing his pockets with it, only sometime between arriving at the house and wandering the rooms, his purpose had changed. He was here for her—his mother. It struck him as funny. Breaking and entering for someone who couldn't even pick him out of a police lineup. He started to laugh again and shook his head, "Hey guys," he began, ready to let them in on the joke, but then a great smarting erupted on one side of his face, and he sunk to the ground.

He woke on a lounge chair in front of furniture that hid the TV, his upper body listing to one side. When he righted his head, a burning sensation slid down his neck. He tried to touch it, but he was tied up, his arms angled behind him, the rest of him fastened to the seat in some way. The place where they'd hit him had swelled, making it difficult to see.

He'd have preferred that they kill him, beat him badly and left him on the side of the road, but this, to be tied to this chair, in this house? He rotated his hands in their noose, tried to turn, but everything held tight, fastened behind him. They had trapped Footer inside his body, and the great irony of it made his jaw quiver. "Get me out of here!" he roared. "Get back here, you bastards!" Let them finish him off. Let them do something, anything more than this. He knew they were still there. Anger riddled his body, and he knew that when this was over, when he was freed, he would be different, changed. This anger—its metallic taste—would remain.

"Bastards!" he called to them. Bastard, he thought, of himself.

Someone approached in the darkness and hit him on the head in the same spot. Pain skidded down his back. He'd play dead like he might have done as a child, goofing around with his mother, crawling over her feet as she made dinner, her slippers shuffling on the linoleum while shooing him away. Good smells rose from the oven, from the soft curve of her hip; she stirred something in a pot with a spoon, then put the spoon down and turned to him; she clapped her hands on her thighs, whistled to him, and their game would begin. "Here puppy! Here pup-pup," she'd say, and he'd scurry up her legs, slip his hands up the ankle of her slacks. He'd be her puppy. He yipped and wagged his behind. She'd ask him to sit, and he'd obey, and she'd pet his head. "Good puppy." Then she'd ask him to beg, and he'd make his back ramrod straight, pull his hands up to his chest, bark. "Good puppy," she'd say again and scratch him behind the ears.

One of the two kicked him in the belly, and Footer tried to cover the hurt with his hands, but they were still fastened behind him; he rolled toward his other side, like she had lain in the snow, alone, waiting for the retired couple to find her on their way home from dinner.

He could feel the chill now and shivered, the snow, it swept across his face, the wind. Fury bubbled inside him, and he pictured himself springing up with his fists, teeth gritted, blood already in his mouth; he started swinging, pummeling them, these two punks, breaking into their house, the home he shared with his mother. Who did they think they were coming here, interrupting their happiness? He thought he could hear her, his mother, preparing dinner in the kitchen. He needed to teach these kids a lesson. "Just a minute, Mom," he said, making a silent promise that everything from this point forward would be for her.

FREDONIA
THE GREAT

I WOKE WITH HIM STANDING OVER ME, could feel the stink of his breath without smelling a thing. He poked me with something sharp. The edge of a knife? Then told me to get up, said we needed to take a little trip. I put one of Borlen's sweatshirts over my nightgown, slipped a pair of jeans under that. A soft glow from the hall propped the room, made it levitate. He stood in the bedroom doorway; tall, he filled the space. I recognized him, one of the Doreghty boys. The oldest one. Couldn't recall his name, but if hard pressed, I could open my record book, find the date of his birth. He watched me with cool interest, and I had to keep myself from opening my mouth, telling him I had stood between his mother's legs as she pushed him out. Ginny Doreghty was a good woman. I wanted him to know this is how I felt about his cancer-riddled mother, but I kept quiet. I put on woolen socks and tied back my graying hair, followed him into the kitchen, where another man in worn denim overalls and a reedy mustache opened and closed cabinet doors, the wood as solid as the day Borlen had crafted them by hand.

It's in the sugar bowl, I told him. He glared at me and then grabbed the bowl from the counter. He drew a handful of bunched bills and threw them on the floor. He snorted in disgust. Then a second later stuffed the bills into his pockets. They had never paid me much for my doctoring. Most people left me a cooler of meat, baked me loaves of bread.

But I had fewer patients now.

Let's go, said Doreghty. I grabbed my medicine bag. They shut the door behind me. I didn't think to wonder when I would be back.

It was mild for November. Kind of a milky humidity. I walked between Doreghty and the man with the overalls.

We hiked down the hillside surrounding my property through leaves that had dropped in last week's storm. I stumbled on a root, caught myself. At one point I put a hand out on the back of Doreghty's T-shirt to keep myself from falling. I wanted to tell him I had known his father and grandfather and that my grandmother had nursed them back from the flu epidemic that gripped Ingleside in the thirties. But I doubted they would take this into account.

The pickup was a battered thing, and the guy in the overalls opened the door for me. I got in, sandwiched between them. The window was cracked, and air whirred into the cabin. Tires crunched along blacktop. Overhead the moon shone a gleaming crescent. We traveled west past the replica gas lamps that lined the streets of downtown Ingleside. In our wake we left Welmann's, Gabe's Diner, and the hardware store I once lived above. We also passed souvenir shops and their blinking signs, front windows jammed with T-shirts and trinkets, lollipops shaped like the Tornado, the famed Glory Days coaster.

I am not a young woman by any means. I didn't worry about my own safety. What was worth living for? I thought of my daughter, Tricia. The last time I had ridden my bike past her apartment, I had noticed that she and her son had decorated their flimsy door with construction paper pumpkins. She had refused to see me for five years now, since Billy was born. It was the only thing

I wanted, I thought, as the truck jerked to a stop on the long gravel drive surrounding the Doreghtys' property. I wanted to be invited into that apartment. I wanted to smell the syrup from Billy's frozen waffles, kiss handfuls of his freckles, pull him onto my lap and read him a storybook.

I wanted him to call me Grandma.

Move it, Fredonia, said Doreghty, motioning outside the truck.

We cut across the field to get to the house. There hadn't yet been a frost, the ground still soft. I moved slowly, my dumb feet unsteady in shoes. The Doreghtys used to farm soybeans and corn when I was a kid, but it had been years since they'd planted a thing.

Every light was on as we climbed the steps to the front porch. I had only been in the Doreghty house once before, and that was years ago, when Ginny delivered her first. I blinked as the door opened, and we stepped inside, light such a brilliant white it reminded me of the new store that sold both food and furniture around the clock in Pruewood. Brightness so unlike anything you could find naturally occurring on God's good earth.

I followed the oldest Doreghty boy down the hall to a wood-paneled back room, where Ginny stretched out on a couch. There were double-hung windows on three of the walls, and I wondered if in better times this had been a sitting parlor, a place to come and watch the sun set over the rows of corn and feel blessed.

Her hair had gone white with the illness, and it stretched out over the sides of her face like wings. I touched Ginny's face with my fingers. We used to go to the same church as children, and I could remember sitting on a rug beside her, two red ribbons at the end of her braids, while Sister Martha read us the story of Noah's Ark, held up a pair of plastic animals with every page she turned.

I searched for Ginny's pulse without success. Her skin was the color of an overripe banana, her breath still. I held a hand above her mouth and then placed my head ear side down on her chest. Nothing. I'm so sorry for your loss, I said.

Fuck that! someone said, another one of the Doreghty boys whom I hadn't noticed in the dimly lit corner. He was short and balding, thicker around the middle than the Doreghty who brought me here. He bashed his fist into the wall, and a piece of plaster the size of an eyeball fell to the ground. He stomped forward, grabbed the shoulder of my sweatshirt, and started shaking me. I could feel the soup I'd had for dinner jostling inside me; his hands, strong and full of vigor, reached out and picked me up.

He let me go, and I felt myself airborne, weightless for a moment, and I recalled how Borlen used to pull me on top of him when we made love, and then I felt this great heaviness followed by the crushing weight of my bones slamming against the window. The shimmering sound of shattering glass. I tasted blood. So this is how it would end.

Then it came to me—Jeremy was the name of the oldest Doreghty boy. He was born in December 1978. The delivery had lasted four and one-half hours from start to finish, and he'd been jaundiced. I'd held him under a tableside lamp myself.

What the fuck? asked Jeremy, pushing his brother clear across the room. Why'd you have to do that?

I brought my hands to my head, tried to steady the ringing. Jeremy helped me up. He seemed concerned. What my brother means is that's not why you're here. I nodded. Tried to focus on his now blurry face. I'm not a dummy.

I don't do visions anymore, I told them. Never was very good at them, I said, thinking about the last vision I'd done and how afterward Tricia hadn't wanted anything to do with me.

It's what we want. It's why we've brought you here, said Jeremy.

Ain't leaving till you lay hands on her, said the shorter brother, his scalp glinting from the overhead light.

You don't understand. I looked at the younger Doreghty, the one who threw me, his stomach heaving over the band of his jeans. He seemed to wield the most power. I don't do it anymore. Can't see a lick. After what I did to Billy, I believed that to be true.

Like hell, he said, and spit out the opening my body had made in the window beside where his mother lay dead.

*

I had always assumed I'd die of a heart attack, just like my grandmother and great-grandmother. I had laid hands on myself long ago, when I was still in my thirties and full of the haughtiness of youth. I'd been perfectly healthy when I did it. Borlen and I were newly married then. He had just started to work on the house that would be our home, where I currently live, and at the time we were living in a tiny apartment above the hardware store. All day we could hear the copper bells ring as people came in to buy their lightbulbs and brooms.

It was a Saturday morning, and the sun strode in the long windows, filled the room with luminous heat. I stretched across Borlen's chest, listened to him breathe, my mind not really dwelling on anything. Borlen lifted my hand from the nest of hair on his chest, fitted his fingers inside my own. He was working construction then on the park and had an afternoon shift later that day.

Would you lay hands on me? he asked, quieter than usual, like he already knew the boundary he was asking me to cross. I laughed and play punched his shoulder, then rearranged the pillow behind my head. I focused on a smudge on the window.

You're serious? I shook my head. I don't want to.

Come on. I want to know.

Well, I don't.

We're all going to die someday, Maureen. It'd be nice to hear from you how it's going to happen.

I was so full of love for him at that point. Drunk on his smell, his touch. My legs were chapped from our long night together, and I thought that nothing could separate us, figured we would go on like that for forty, fifty, sixty years.

The foolishness of youth.

Okay, I said, and gathered my nightgown in one hand. I straddled him. My hair flowed over my shoulders like a cape. I placed my hands palm down on his chest, could feel my eyes rolling back while the rest of me remained steady. I saw the sky, a deep cerulean blue, and I was Borlen atop the steel structure of a roller coaster. The wind coursed against the scruff of his neck as he bent over a metal beam, worked on one of two inversions for the coaster; a visor covered his face, and blue sparks shimmered in a generous arc on either side of him. I saw a wisp of his brown hair, noticed his unlined face, and it puzzled me. His youthfulness.

Borlen's stomach grumbled as he welded. As a boy, his mother would fill a thermos with tomato soup, and hours later he'd open it at his desk in school and watch the steam rise. How glorious it had been to see his mother's face when he stepped off the bus at the end of the day and she leaned down, pulled him into her. Sometimes Maureen reminded him of his mother, the way she might touch his arm absently, like a breeze, and then it was Maureen's moony face he thought of, and he was kissing her that first time outside the entrance to McKinley Park, bumblebees circling; she tasted of strawberries and Cokes, and when he flicked his tongue against hers, he felt a liquid heat rise up from the base of him and spread out. He could feel her inside him—in the back of his throat, beneath the calluses on his fingers. And he wanted to keep kissing her, didn't think he'd ever be able to stop himself from pressing his lips against hers.

There was a blast of pain at the base of his neck. An errant beam had loosened from above him and swung away, and Borlen toppled head first over the steel skeleton where he worked.

Borlen reached out toward the structure. Wind cupped his body as he fell.

My lover. My love, I thought, breath all caught up in my throat. The blood that rushed through my veins seemed to come to a standstill. Everything I had assumed about us and our life together had shattered. I rolled off him, returned to my side of the bed. Tried to compose myself.

What'd you see? Borlen wanted to know. A car crash? Cancer?

My pulse raced, and I was not certain if it was the breaking of my heart or the customary thrill of laying hands. I couldn't see much, I told him. Just saw some birds, felt myself sail through the sky.

You aren't being honest, Mo. I know you too well. Tell me. But I refused to speak, turned from him. I'm not gonna beg you, he said. Maybe you didn't see anything. Maybe I'm the guy that'll live forever. The first.

I smiled for him. Kissed his mouth and then went into the bathroom. I locked the door and sat on the tub ledge. I held myself as tight as I could. Willed out the image of Borlen falling. I pulled my hair, rocked back and forth, then cursed my stupidity. And then I laid hands on myself. I'd tried many times before without success. It would work this time. I just needed to figure out how to make it happen the same moment as Borlen. We would die together, I told myself, drying my face, pulling back my hair. It was the only way I could get myself to reach for the doorknob and go on.

*

The younger Doreghty, the thick balding one, brought me a glass of water. I guessed that was his version of an apology, and I was ready to accept it because I was suddenly thirsty. He also placed a sleeve of crackers on the table beside me. I held the glass with both hands and drank the whole thing. I thanked him, and he nodded. We were coming to a sort of understanding. Don't yell or shout, and they won't tie me up.

My jaw had swelled up real nice from when they first brought me here, and he thought he could just beat a vision out of me. Be my guest, I could have said. You think it's a blessing to see things no one else can see? To be a witness to death? If Doreghty or anybody else wanted to end this for me, I would not fight them.

The sky was now a dusty gray, the air bitter and still. From where I sat, I could see that Ginny's nail beds had gone blue. They taped a garbage bag over the broken window, and the plastic billowed back and forth with the wind. The water revived me, set my own blood to a quicker pace, and I asked if I could go to the bathroom. Didn't say it to anyone in particular, but a girlfriend appeared. She didn't look much older than eighteen, and I wanted to know what she was doing with these monkeys. I wondered where her parents were, why she wasn't in school reading books and memorizing facts. But for once I kept quiet. She led me to a small bathroom with pink flowered wallpaper that could use a good scrubbing. I heard the floorboards on the other side of the door as I relieved myself, and it made me smile to think that she was watching me, as if what I once had was worth protecting. I started the faucet, turned the blue-and-white bar in my hands, and it reminded me of all the times I've scrubbed to examine a patient—to guide a baby into the world or to help someone leave it.

The girl knocked and told me to finish up. I couldn't find a towel. Dried my hands on the bottom of Borlen's sweatshirt and opened the door. You need anything else? she asked.

I smiled at her. I like you, I wanted to say. I could see myself at eighteen, setting broken bones, the memory of my grandmother's hands guiding me. I thanked the girl, and she led me back to my chair outside Ginny's room, only I didn't sit down. I walked up to Ginny. I undid the sheet they'd pulled over her face. I could feel the girlfriend watching me. You gonna lay hands? she asked. I bent to Ginny's ear. You've done good. Your boys are here. You go and do what you need to do.

Someone pushed what felt like a gun between my shoulder blades, and then I heard a zapping sound. Pain traveled down my arms and legs, and some sort of electrical current forced me to lose all ability to stand. I fell onto the ground in a heap. Beneath Ginny's bed I could see balls of dust, a stack of waterlogged phone books and newspapers.

You ain't calling the shots here, lady, said the balding Doreghty. He stood above me. You do what I say when I say it. There was a shoe in the middle of my back, my jaw tight against the floor. I felt the pressure of my own heart ramming away in my chest. Dear God I was ready.

You're as much of a pussy now as you ever were, I spat. And then I waited for the snap and pop of my neck. Waited to again feel Borlen's arms around me.

*

I'm not altogether proud of how I've managed. If I could do it over, I would have let the visions pass through me like water in a sieve. I would have kept quiet. But I was proud, see? I felt special. I am a Fredonia. Our lineage of healing in Ingleside can be traced back more than two hundred years. We could set bones, make a compress to stop a migraine, mix a tea to urge a uterus to hold onto a baby or let one slip away. Yet I was different. I could see into the future, the final moments most people dreaded. I shared this with them, made something feared familiar.

My grandmother would have thought it foolish theatrics. You do that on your own time, she might have said of my hand laying. But she never experienced it—seeing death well in advance. Initially, I could only see visions in the living, and then one night it all changed, became so much more complicated.

It was never the same after that.

I was riding my bike after a house call and was a few miles from the home I shared with Borlen when I saw the flashing lights, the flapping yellow police tape. Brittany Vogel had been missing from Ingleside for nearly two weeks. She was nine years old, and in the photo of her that ran in the *Ingleside Courier*, her red hair hung as straight as uncooked spaghetti. They found her face down on the bank of the Black River, seven miles south of where she'd last been spotted. She was only wearing tennis shoes, and they were tied on the wrong feet.

I slid off my bike, leaned it against a tree. It was late May, and the Black River spun in a brown churl. I called out, asked if anyone required medical attention. I remember police tape bobbing, the flash of cameras, someone taking my picture. A tent constructed out of tarps. Large boxes of light were fixed on stands. I saw her hand first, the water lapping the slight bend of her fingers. The sky shone a pearly purple beneath the heavy moon, and because of it, I could see the glimmer of chipped polish on her fingernails. I was as familiar in town as the courthouse, and they partially uncovered her as I approached.

She was only a baby really. Her belly still round like a drum. Her skin was parched, pulled tight across her bones. She was already dead, but as I crouched beside Brittany, something told me to touch her. When I placed my hands beneath her bent collarbone, my eyes rolled back, and I was transported.

No one could have been more surprised than me.

She had been thinking about her bed at home with its fairy-printed comforter, imagining that she had caught a butterfly in a net, an orange butterfly with black and yellow spots. She heard the muted sounds of her parents downstairs. She could just make out the music from a show on TV and the smell of buttered popcorn. She brushed her feet back and forth beneath the sheets, liked the feel of them; she could smell her mother's hair conditioner on her own damp locks. During bath her mother had said, Okay, just this once, before putting the white dollop in her palm and rubbing it into Brittany's hair.

Then she was crying. Great rollicking tears slid down Brittany's cheeks. She was barefoot in a basement, wearing only her bathing suit, a rainbow-colored thing with pink ruffled straps. She shivered. From cold or fear or a combination of the two. There was a man with her. Oversized, his eyes sunk in his cheeks like pits in rotten fruit. He was running his hands down her naked arms and legs. His hands were wet. Sticky. Brittany cried harder, said, Please, Mommy. Please come, Mommy.

But the man—he didn't want her to cry. Told her to be quiet. Didn't like loud sounds. Overhead the floorboards squealed.

Maybe it was Mommy and Daddy and her brother and sister and the police, she thought. He shushed her, moved his fingers with greater force. It had been hours since they'd met at the pool, and now her suit was wet, and when she felt the wetness trickle down her legs, she knew she'd peed, which made her yell even louder for her mother and the green tiled bathroom where her mother would take off her wet clothes and pat her dry with a thick towel. On the bathroom wall in their house was the framed picture of a turtle taking a bubble bath. His hands, the man's hands. He had a name. Brittany knew his name. He had told her several times, but it was gone gone gone.

Mommy, she called. Then thought the word, saw the letters lining up in her mind, great black soldiers that would rescue her with their sharpened bayonets and take her home, feed her a peanut butter and jelly sandwich, pour her glass after glass of the coldest milk; a great grasp tightened around her neck, and everything became ultra vivid for a moment, maybe three, her mother's face—Brittany saw her mother's eyes all crinkled up with laughter, her soft mouth open, pink tongue nestled between teeth. What's so funny, Mommy? Brittany wondered. Tell me.

*

Borlen died that fall, but his seed had already made a home in me, and as much as I wanted to follow Borlen, I still had that part of him inside me and was determined to see it through. I forced down every orange and bite of apple. Swallowed my own snot as I ate a chunk of cheese, a slice of cucumber. I can't tell you how many times I mixed the herbs for tea that would sufficiently end it for both of us. Cried the whole time I did it. Went so far to boil water, let the poultice steep in the steaming mug. I always turned it over in the sink.

After laying hands on Brittany Vogel, I helped reconstruct her final moments, which led to a sketch of the man and his eventual conviction. My phone rang all day with offers from the FBI and the police and those who'd recently lost loved ones. Eventually, I yanked the phone from the wall and tossed it across the room. When they came to my door begging for the final visions of their dead brothers and sisters and spouses, fanning crisp one hundred dollar bills beneath my door, I crouched in the hallway where no one could see me. Even went so far to load Borlen's rifle, aim it toward the door where they pleaded their requests.

In the meantime I grew big in the house Borlen had built for us. Walked barefoot across the planks he'd hewn and varnished a deep walnut. I memorized every knot on our kitchen table, felt the way his hands must have grown warm as he sanded the posts for our bed, that sacred place. I lathered my face and used his razor, memorized the feel of the blade on my skin. Took every flannel and pair of pants he'd owned and heaped it on the bed, slept with the feel of his clothes nested around me. I slipped on Borlen's waders, went down to where the river widens a mile or so from the dam, and stood there in that brackish water with Borlen's fishing pole, and all the while I grew. I could place a hand on my belly where part of Borlen was alive, swimming safely inside me.

I gave birth to Tricia on a cold and wet day in March. I had felt her sinking down, getting into position for weeks. I lined the bathtub with clean blankets, placed around me everything I might possibly need. But it didn't matter how many successful births I'd been a part of—I wasn't quite prepared for the way the pain clamped down, held me asunder. I cursed Borlen. I cursed God himself and all the glory of heaven as I pushed and panted, felt the tip of Tricia's head against my fingers, glimpsed a sliver of Borlen's dark hair in a mirror I held between my legs. And then I felt an urge to push until my eyes turned inside out, and I shat in my own tub, and the great mercy of the child flooded out into my near-limp hands.

I cleared her mouth and listened as her piercing cry filled our bathroom. I sunk down in my own stink, wrapped Tricia in a soft blanket, and held the beauty as Borlen's last breaths grazed the inside of my arm.

*

Tricia was slow to speak, but when she finally did, she spoke in full sentences. She was nearly three years old by then, and we were broke. We'd used up the money from Borlen's insurance policy, and the few broken bones and illnesses I'd agreed to treat were not enough to cover our accumulating bills. We had been eating oatmeal for days when I poured the last bit of milk into Tricia's cup and looked around the room. I thought of how Borlen had taken care of me, how he had worked every Saturday because the pay was good, had roused himself in darkness to drive to the city, where he could earn double. I opened the phone book and called the main number for the amusement park, asked to speak to one of the higher-ups at Glory Days. Finally, they connected me with the director of marketing. After I explained who I was and what I could do for them, the director became excited. I told her I could make Glory Days popular beyond anything she could imagine. Two days later she sent a limo to our house. I never did learn how to drive. Tricia wore a black corduroy dress with white tights, patent leather shoes. Her hair trickled flat over her shoulders as we sat in the backseat and practiced flashcards I had made with different pictures of *R* and *S* words. To her *sand* was pronounced *thand*, *seashore* morphed into *thee*. Tricia referred to a fluffy rabbit as a "wabbit" and wouldn't even attempt to say the word *ribbon*. We worked on the cards during the drive. But after five minutes she took them from my hands and made them into a fan. Should we practice some more? I asked.

No.

Okay, I said. That's fine. I placed my hands in my lap and tried to prepare for this new venture.

Upon our arrival they introduced me to the president of Glory Days and several other men dressed in suits. Their faces were grim, and they kept checking their watches. Meanwhile, the director of marketing buzzed around. She talked about offering the guests of Glory Days a one-of-a-kind experience. She mentioned a California zoo where guests could spend the night with an animal and an amusement park in Nashville where you could dance onstage with a life-sized hologram of Elvis. She showed charts, discussed revenue. The president yawned. She was blowing it.

I can show you! I announced, pushing back from the table where we sat. I looked from one face to the next and then gathered Tricia from where she played under the table. She was lean, maybe thirty pounds then. She never wanted to finish her milk, said it tasted itchy. I laid her out on the table, and she giggled. I didn't think much about it. We needed the money. Believe me when I say that. When it all started, I was only thinking of the paycheck and how it would keep food on the table.

Be still now, sweetie. I told the men to form a circle around me and to hold hands, and then I told the marketing director and the president to put their hands on my shoulders.

Tricia wiggled around, and I tried to tell her with a look that this was serious. Maybe a better mom wouldn't have made the choice I did or would have thought through the consequences. Instead, I placed hands on her. I felt the familiar spinning, only this time it was Tricia that I saw. She was older—in her late thirties—and her hair streaked with gray. She huddled in the corner of a room in a stained shirt. Her face was swollen. Everything about her looked unnatural, not right. Her eyes were closed, and blood leaked from the top of her head, disguised part of her face. A man stood over her. She lifted a hand to protect herself, but the man—mean faced, overgrown brows, greasy haired, with a Tweety Bird tattoo on his arm—screamed at her. That all you got?

He would not be stopped. The man drew back his leg and kicked her in the side with his boot. She slunk further to the floor. That's right. No more? That's it?

Her eyes remained closed, lips dry and scaly—yet I was the one she saw. In her final moments we were together eating ice cream from cones, then picking strawberries one warm June day—one berry for the bucket, the other for the mouth. And then I was giving her a bubble bath, and she pretended to pour me tea. A bad dream in the middle of the night, and I lifted her from her warm bed, held her in my arms, made her comfortable again.

When I finished, the marketing director's face had gone white. The president mumbled an apology and then cleared his throat. Miss Fredonia, he said, taking my hand and shaking it. You are going to be a great star. I looked down at Tricia. She was playing with the buckle on her shoe. I patted her head, smiled dimly.

I held Tricia on my lap during the short drive home and worked my fingers through the straight planes of her hair. Traced the skin of her cheek. Wept. She played with the ashtrays while I cried at what I now knew.

*

The Doreghtys undid the sheet from Ginny's face, gathered around her and held hands. They didn't say anything when I joined them. Her skin had taken on a bluish pallor, mouth slightly ajar. It was late, during the wee hours of morning, and outside there was nothing but the glow of the moon, a brilliant expanse of stars, a light near the pole barn. Ginny had refused radiation, all the modern treatments the city doctors offered. When they wanted to transfer her to a hospice in Savoy, she had refused.

They all told Ginny they loved her, bent down and kissed her cheek. She'd birthed three boys. She knew how to till the land, drive a tractor, dress a chicken, and feed a family. I wanted to tell them that there is joy in such a full life.

After a prolonged pause, the shorter Doreghty nudged me forward. He went so far as to withdraw my hands from my pockets and place them close to Ginny's chest. We just want to know what she was feeling, said Jeremy. We weren't always close. Can't say we've always been kind. But we love her. His eyes became wet. We just need to know she was okay. Felt loved and all that.

Of course she did, I said.

Then show us. Do this one thing, and we'll let you go.

I shook my head. I'd like to help. I would. But I can't.

You won't. Be truthful.

I won't. I felt nothing but the room's cold air, the orange buzz of a space heater in the corner. I made sure her eyelids were firmly closed. Pulled the sheet up around Ginny's shoulders. I wasn't certain what else I could do. When Borlen died, I didn't want to see anyone, didn't want to do anything but mourn who and what he'd been. Ginny had been dying for weeks, and yet their grief seemed unwieldy. Still, I touched Jeremy's elbow and said what I wished someone might have taken the time to say to me: You did all that you could.

*

I was haunted by what I knew about Tricia's end. I glimpsed her battered form as I washed dishes or brushed my teeth. Again and again I saw the face of the guy standing over her, the one with the tattoo. I saw him take his leg back, saw the toe of his boot meet her body. I was determined to keep him at bay. I installed double locks on our doors and had all the windows wired for an alarm. I arranged my schedule at Glory Days so I spent every other night at home. The evenings I wasn't there, I hired a sitter. Tricia loved school. She earned good grades, and her teachers never failed to tell me that she was a leader. But she returned crying on more than one occasion, said that the kids forced her hands on them and mocked her when she didn't have anything to say.

I can't do anything, she wailed.

You're a gift, Tricia. Just being here is a gift.

She shook off my hands. I want to do something. I want a special power.

Honey, I'll help you work toward any dream that you have. But this. This is not a dream. Laying hands is a job.

But you can teach me.

I'm sorry, I said. I can't.

Meanwhile, word spread. Billboards advertised Fredonia the Great as far away as Erie, Pennsylvania. In them I wore a gold turban and laid hands on an attractive young woman as her family circled us. Fredonia dolls and replica turbans crammed gift shop windows. They built me my own venue with an air-conditioned waiting area, a row of benches, and windows on either side. Velvet sashes marked the entrance to my chamber. Inside was a bed-like table where guests stretched out, and as soon as they lifted their feet, placed their heads on matching velour pillows, the light dimmed. The music grew hushed. The lines for my services sometimes lasted three or four hours in length, and the park gave me my own security guards. It was flattering. There were photo shoots and autograph signings and raffles for charities. Sometimes the newspapers would follow me to the local nursing home or the hospital—places where death lurked and I was able to offer a friendly face.

At home I seldom had to ask Tricia to clean her room or take out the garbage. She did her homework, excelled in every subject, especially math. Tricia was obedient to a fault except when it came to my work. She begged me to stay home with her or teach her how to lay hands. When she got older, she pleaded for us to leave Ingleside, to move somewhere new. Don't you like it here? I asked.

It's fine, she'd say.

We could go anywhere, I said, but I spoke without conviction. I was earning such good money. Another year or two, honey, and we'll move on, I told her. But in all honesty, how could I leave Ingleside? The Fredonias had been a mainstay for more than two centuries. I really couldn't imagine myself anywhere else.

Somewhere in the middle of it, she grew up, and despite what I knew about her future, by the time I tried to change, it was too late. I started to cut back my hours so that Tricia and I could go to the city for the weekend and see a show or visit a museum, but she'd politely decline. She said she had homework. I had no reason not to believe her. Sometimes I'd return home, and her bedroom door would be locked, and I'd stand outside it and knock, ask if she wanted some tea.

I'm busy, Mom. No thanks, she'd say.

I only worked a few days by then, had grown tried of the demands on my time and skills. Sometimes I was able to be home when she returned from school, and I peppered her with questions. I wanted to know who she saw, what they spoke about. You know you can talk to me. She rolled her eyes. Never mind, I said. And even though she was standing right in front of me, it felt like she was miles away.

I returned to the Fredonia journals, searched for a cure to her ailing spirits. In the process I again began to cultivate the garden. It was spring, and I could smell the sun in the air. Sometimes Tricia would come outside and sit on the picnic table Borlen had made for us. It seemed like she was waiting for someone, something. I talked about the lavender and alfalfa I was planting, showed her how to split open a pod to extract a seed, explained how to roast it over an open flame then cool it, press it into a powder. I reminded her that she was a Fredonia: Your grandmother, great-grandmother, and great-great-grandmother were healers. It's in your blood.

I know, she'd say, unmoved.

Would you like to learn some of their treatments? She'd shrug. Tricia?

Not really.

She turned sixteen a few weeks later, and I made her a cake in the shape of a rabbit, something I might have done for her when she was a toddler. She smiled out of kindness. Kissed my cheek and then said the cake needed whiskers and started rummaging through the pantry. It had been a long time since she'd touched me, and with her kiss I recalled how as a child she used to pull on the end of my nose. In the middle of the night she would call my name, stand in the middle of her crib and stretch her arms toward me. I didn't know where the time had gone or what I had to show for it.

One morning I woke before the sun. Something was not right. I walked through the house, checked the locks on the doors, and peered outside to see if anything looked unusual. And then I made my way down the hall, opened the door to her room and saw him there, his bare arm tossed casually over her breasts. He looked around twenty, his face gaunt but heavy with stubble. The tattoo of a grinning Tweety Bird flaunted his bicep.

I grabbed a polka-dotted frame Tricia's friends had given her for her birthday and held it up. It took all my might to refrain from breaking it over his head—my arms and hands shook, my jaw trembled. Get the hell out! I yelled.

What? His eyes were hazy, booze wafted off him.

Mommy, what are you doing? Tricia grabbed at the blankets to cover herself. He pulled on his pants, opened the bedroom window, and slipped outside. I yelled, Don't you dare step foot in this house again. I mean it!

They called him Footer. Footer Portman. I had seen him before along the river, under the viaduct on 200 South with a group of dropouts. When I asked Tricia what she was doing, she told me to chill out. I could smell that she'd been smoking. We're just friends, she said.

Friends? You don't get in a bed with friends.

You're overreacting. We were just sleeping. Really. A few minutes later I heard water from the shower on full blast.

But Footer did return a few nights later, and this time I was ready. I cracked open the door to Tricia's room and lingered with my rifle upright across my chest, finger on the trigger. Her cheekbone rested against the bulb of his shoulder and the balsam color of her hair. It could have been Borlen and me dozing—and really, it should have been us. Watching her there with him, her lover, my belly twisted. She had what I wanted. What I'd never stopped wanting.

I bent over my knees to clear my head and then righted myself. I aimed the gun at Footer's head and told him to get up, said if I ever saw his greasy ass in my house, I'd blow him to pieces, so help me God.

Just save it, Mom. Tricia pulled a sweatshirt over her head. We're leaving.

Don't you dare! What could I say, what could I do? I stood in the doorway as they headed out. Tricia! I called. I saw your vision. I laid hands on you long ago—I ran up to her. It isn't pretty. Please stay. I'll keep you safe.

She stopped and looked at me with venom. I'll be fine, she said. I stood there in my bedclothes and naked feet and watched her go.

*

At dawn, before the coffee had even brewed, the Doreghty boys pulled on stocking caps, gathered shovels from the shed, and told me to follow them. They gave me a pair of men's work gloves and a jacket that I eagerly zipped. It couldn't have been more than thirty degrees outside and damp with the previous day's rain. My breath clouded above me. The ground had frosted, and the grasses bent like spears through clumps of frozen mud. We walked what seemed to be the length of the Doreghty property, a good quarter-mile southwest. The sky grew brighter, and I thought what a pretty day for Ginny to be buried. We climbed a slight incline to a plot with a mulberry tree. From the raised bed I could see the two brooks that knotted together to form the Black River. On the other side stood the Doreghtys' white farmhouse, the sheds and old barn from which we'd come.

As we dug our shovels into the earth, a reddish orange spot appeared on the horizon, then later faded until the sky took on a grayish hue. Sweat dribbled down my neck. I unzipped the jacket to let in fresh air. The Doreghty boys were steady in their work. They did not pause to talk or take a break. I thought there might be tears, recollections, but their eyes were steely, mouths set.

By the time we finished digging Ginny's grave, it was likely noon, and my stomach ached. I hadn't thought of food at all since the Doreghtys had brought me to their farm, but with my presence no longer necessary, I could suddenly taste a real breakfast of scrambled eggs with bits of potato and green pepper, a few crumbles of bacon mixed in, just like Borlen used to make us on Sundays. On those days we'd stay in bed for hours, drink cup after cup of the blackest coffee, share pieces of buttered toast from the same plate.

Mentally, I opened the refrigerator door and counted the eggs, peered inside the drawer where I kept the vegetables. I wondered if perhaps I still had a few slabs of bacon in the freezer. I'd sauté an onion first, that's how Borlen did it. Beat the eggs with a dollop of cream, a dash of pepper.

It had been a long time since Borlen was here, since someone made me a meal, I was thinking, when they pointed to the grave and told me to get in. I looked at them. Trained my eyes on Jeremy a good head or two above his pit bull of a brother. It's deep enough, if that's what you're wondering, I said.

The shorter one snorted. You think you're so smart, dontcha lady. You think you can just keep all your secrets to yourself like we don't have a right. Like they aren't ours.

His face was red, nostrils sharp and prominent. I could feel hatred radiate off his body from where he stood on the other side of the grave.

But it was Jeremy. The hands that had taken Ingleside High School to the football playoffs two years in a row in the mid-nineties reached out, grabbed me by the scruff of my coat, sent me sailing into Ginny's grave.

*

I knew they were staying along the river, living with Footer in a tent beneath the viaduct along with his friends. The first time Tricia let me hold her son, it was winter, and fires whipped from metal garbage cans. Billy was only a few months old then, but already I could tell there was something wrong with his leg. It remained still, nearly flat in the blanket I'd brought. There are so many things that can go wrong in a delivery. Even now I think it could have been worse. Tricia seemed better than I'd seen her in years, and she gave me the briefest of hugs. We'd lived apart for over a year, but motherhood had softened her. She seemed pleased to see me. I didn't glimpse Footer, and I wondered if she was finally ready to come home.

She handed my grandson to me, and I was supposed to check his vitals, palpate the leg. Yet my purpose for being there slipped away. It felt so good to hold Billy, to fill my arms with him. I placed a hand against the fine hair at the back of his head, and everything that I missed came to me at once—the love of a good man, the neediness of a child. What did I have? I rocked Billy back and forth, brushed my knuckles against his cheeks, breathed the cave of air between his shoulder and jaw. How I wished that he were mine and that I could take him back to the home Borlen had built.

Tricia snatched him from me. You can't hog him. He has lots of mamas, she said, and she tripped over that final letter *S*, reminding me of the early years we had spent working on her speech. Sure enough, Billy was passed from hand to hand; one woman even pulled up her shirt to nurse him. I stood there. My face burned. And then I tipped my chin up. Spoke.

Do you want me to lay hands on him?

Tricia's expression skewed, looked uncertain. I don't know that I want that information. She kissed his dimpled cheek.

Yes! said a woman who held a sleeping toddler in her arms.

Please, I said, I'd love to do this for you. Come on, Tricia. It will be fun.

I looked from her clear face to those of her friends, soot stained and smelling of campfire and unwashed hair. Okay. Tricia unfolded the blanket I had brought and placed it on the ground. She took Billy from her friend and laid him on his back in the middle of it, told me to go ahead.

I wanted them to accept me. I wanted to be asked back. I was Fredonia the Great. They couldn't buy what I offered. I slipped my fingers beneath his blankets until I felt skin, then felt the familiar rolling back, drifting away. Tricia's friends, five women and one pimpled teenage boy, joined hands, and then the two closest to me placed hands on my shoulders. And then I was little Billy sitting on a blanket in the grass, crawling and stopping to pick up a rock and suck on it. It was cold. Salty. Felt good against his gums. He pulled up onto his knees and then tumbled back over. Wondered where his mommy was, the woman with the eyes. She would hold him against her, her hair tickling his chin. Someone else came and picked him up, jostled him on her hip. But the rock. The pebble. It slipped. Slid from the place where he held it against his tongue. Jammed. Stuck in his throat. The woman called him Cutie Pie and danced with him in a circle. Someone roasted a bird. He smelled the meat. His eyes teared, and his face became hot. Something was not right. The air in his mouth jammed. Went no farther. He waved his arms, and someone swooped down, leaned him over her thigh and whacked his back. If it were his mother, he wished she would turn him over so he could again see her face, and then everything darkened and grew still.

The group that had formed around the blanket where Billy lay grew somber. How dare you, Tricia said. Her eyes narrowed. After all, she was my daughter. She knew me better than anyone. Suddenly Tricia threw herself onto me, and the soft weight left over from the baby pressed against me. You can't come here and tell me this. Can't bring all your bitterness here and destroy my son's life. I won't let you do to him what you did to me.

It was a stupid thing to do, and I regretted it. Tricia pushed herself up from me and lifted Billy into her arms. He made a sweet cooing sound, waved his chubby baby fists. I felt cold stares from the campers, and as I remained there, a warm globule of spit hit my forehead. I let it wend its way into my hair as someone asked, What kind of mother are you?

*

I clawed at the dirt walls of the grave. It filled the sleeves of my jacket, clouded my nostrils and eyes. I couldn't get a handhold. I could only see that white muted sky overhead, a few inches of a tree branch. A chill pierced my bones. My ankle was broken in two places, and when I put weight on it, pain rocketed up my leg. I beat the walls with my fists.

It was dark, and a soft rain had begun to fall. My throat was scraped raw from screaming when I heard someone approach. It was the girlfriend. I knew it before I saw her face.

She flashed a lantern over the grave, and I hopped upright, winced. They said they'd let you out if you lay hands on Ginny, she said. Before too much time passes. They've called the funeral home. They're on their way over. You do it this once, and I'll take you home myself. They said that'd be fine. She placed the lantern on the ground, got on her knees, and stretched her hands toward me. The pads of her fingers were a soft pink and full of life. I stared at them, and as much as I wanted to sit down, draw my knees to my chest and wait for those first few shovels of dirt to splatter my head, I didn't. Couldn't.

*

I'm done with Glory Days. I've told them again and again that Fredonia the Great is no more and that I'm retiring for good. Yet they keep calling, and I keep going. I tell myself it's time to do other things. I want to spend all day weeding the garden behind my house, tending to the horehound, harvesting the nettle and alfalfa and lemon balm that make an excellent digestive aid. I could spend hours yanking the ragweed and then fertilizing with a mixture of eggshell and coffee grounds, working this into the soil.

It's been years now, but I haven't forgotten the days the Doreghtys kept me, nor have I forgiven myself for giving into their wants. But I did it for them—Tricia and Billy. They live only a few miles down the road, and as the loamy earth slips through my fingers, the sun on my back, I push the past away and dream.

Birds call to one another, flit from branch to branch, and I feel okay. Better than okay. Hopeful. And when that feeling arrives, I move quickly, brush the dirt from my hands, put on a clean shirt, wrap a loaf of zucchini bread in foil and place it in the front basket of my bike. Then I ease onto the seat and push off toward Tricia's. It takes me longer to bike there now; my ankle never did heal right. But once I get there, I imagine Tricia opening the door to her apartment and greeting me with a smile. She will put on a pot of coffee and cut the zucchini bread in thick slices and place them on a plate. Then the two of us will stand on the tiny concrete balcony that overlooks the parking lot and just beyond that a swing set. We will marvel over Billy as he pumps his legs back and forth, holding tight to the chain as he swings higher and higher, his head erect like any other five-year-old. Not saying it, but she will be thinking how wrong my vision about him was. I'll want to ask if she's seeing anyone and remind her not to trust any of the guys around town. But I won't. I'll keep quiet.

Billy! Tricia will yell in her shaky vibrato, God knows what she's on. It's your grandma! she will yell, and I will feel my heart soar. He will step down from the swing, and a smile will eclipse his face. In my mind I will watch him walk, that slender vine of a leg trailing behind him, those special high-tops he wears, but I can't keep the image going—she'll never let me see Billy in her lifetime. The future is beyond our control, Borlen used to say. Billy. I think his name. Imagine tucking him in at night. I know my only hope is to wait her out, let her be her own ruin. This time, I think, I'll get it right.

FOOTER

THE COP INSTRUCTS LUANN TO OPEN HER PURSE just inside the entrance to Glory Days. *I've seen you with that guy*, the cop says. *Don't much like the looks of him.* At this point Luann understands little about Footer's part in the park robberies. For seventeen years she goes along at home and at school—nose too thick, dark, unruly curls in a town of straight-haired beauties. She isn't interesting enough to be noticed. And then that summer Footer chooses her.

It's not like that, she wants to say to the cop. What she and Footer have goes deeper. Blood maybe. *You get into trouble*, the cop says, worming a finger along the inside of her arm. *I can help.*

She jerks her arm away. Someone pushes her forward as another group descends. Luann is not pretty in the way of other girls. Yet this cop, like most men in town, seems to know her—how they stare at her from the corners of their eyes, a dull compression. The attention fills her, but it is an empty fill, like eating cake mix from the box, and she follows along—in the bed of a pickup, on a dirty afghan along the river, underneath the rafters of an abandoned barn, or inside the car of the umbrella ride at Glory Days, where she spends each sweaty evening. When she goes with the men, there's nothing to say. They move together, and there is a kind of wholeness that arrives but never lasts. When it's over, she turns away to arrange her clothes, the blankness on her face. It is nice to be wanted, even if it only lasts a few minutes. But there is no pretending with Footer.

July in Ingleside. River low and motionless. Brook trout disappear, but the frogs multiply tenfold with their deep throaty cries. Only a few farms are left, but corn pollen still thicks the air with its fertile rotting. Luann lives with her grandmother in a falling-down house on a county road, while her dad, Teensy, drives a tractor-trailer across country and back. He is gone a week at a time. Nearly every night Luann squeezes outside her bedroom window and hitches a ride to Glory Days, where there is always someone willing to pay her admittance.

Footer tells her he grew up in Pruewood and is the last of nine. His parents white haired and slow moving. He was an accident, he says. She nods. Understands the importance of knowing where you're from. She's sitting on the stool behind the counter where he works the Gangster Shootout in the Roaring Twenties section of the park. He's dressed in a T-shirt meant to look like a single-breasted suit and wears sunglasses in hours-gone sun. A small tattoo of Tweedy Bird covers his bicep. For a dollar he hands over a toy rifle, instructs a guest to shoot three bottles of bootleg whiskey for a chance to win a stuffed animal.

You're not from here either, he says, and Luann, who's been twisting the stool in a slow swivel stops.

What makes you say that? she asks. Luann's eyeliner is dark. She has on her bikini top, a button-down shirt tied at the waist over that. Her hair springs all over her face in the night's moist heat.

It's written all over you. He gestures to her from head to toe. You're not like these other nincompoops.

I don't know why you'd say that, she says, secretly thrilled at his confidence—at what he might see in her that others are unable to recognize. She doesn't talk about her past with anyone.

Yet all along she has been looking for someone to discern the truth—to see her and understand that she is not of this place. Luann has memorized the paper in Teensy's safe deposit box. Father unknown. She could be the daughter of a movie star or politician, a banker—and is certain she is already more than the rest of the losers in this dead-end town. When Footer says they should go to the city for the night, she agrees. She likes Footer's muscles—how solid he looks. It is summer. What else is there to do? A few hours later they mix Coke and rum in the front seat during the two-hour drive north.

Your birthfather comes here sometimes, Footer says as he parks the car alongside a place called Ned's Watering Hole. This causes her to pause. She figures he must be making this up. He wants to get into her pants, she reasons, no different from any other guy.

Oh, really? she says, slamming the car door. What else do you know about him? 'Cause I don't even know his name.

Inside the bar Footer pats the seat beside him. Orders them drinks. After he takes a long gulp, he speaks. Your first day on earth was almost your last, he says. Your birthfather's name is Kincaid, and he has sent me here to find you. A shiver chitters down Luann's spine, and she's afraid to look away.

Footer says her parents were poorer than most and that they lived like wild animals in an abandoned hunting cabin not far from the river. They feasted on seeds and nuts, creatures that slithered in the grass. Your mother grew large with you while the rest of her shriveled up, until at the end she could no longer walk, and your father lifted her and held her legs on the riverbank. You slid into the water like a fish, nearly swam past his hands.

You're making that up, she says.

Am I?

He acts like he knows so much about her, but Luann knows he's full of it, just like all the others. Still, the air is hot and sticky, and the way he speaks—his sureness—it's unlike anyone else. Dust from the fields creases Luann's fingers, soils the sandals she favors. What harm could come from playing along?

She thinks about what she knows to be true: the home for wayward girls in Chicago, the adoption papers in Teensy's safe deposit box. But Footer's story is more interesting. Luann toys with the idea that it could be true. She's always considered herself better than the other kids—why not imagine her beginning in this way?

By the time they get back to Ingleside, it's nearly morning, and the air is pearly and thin. They stand outside the long trailers behind Glory Days, where the summer help sleeps four to a room. Shh, he says. Luann follows him up three plywood stairs. A bulb hangs from some wires. He holds open the door to his bedroom. Moonlight burns through a rectangular window near the ceiling, and she sees two sets of bunk beds on either wall. A desk stands between the beds. Footer guides her to the bottom bunk on the right. She hears the sounds of the other boys sleeping and slides her hands beneath his shirt.

Footer grabs her wrists, pulls her away. I want to be like your brother, he whispers. Luann smells Footer's beery breath. She eyes the length of hair at the back of his neck, wants to part the strands with her fingers. Okay, she says. What does she have to lose? Maybe she has a brother. Maybe she can pretend he is Footer.

As if he senses her doubts, he speaks. I remember hearing about your first winter, he says. Snow twenty feet deep. Your real daddy secured his feet with newspaper and duct tape. Walked around like a mummy. Kept you inside his shirt. Mixed formula in gas stations. If he couldn't find that, he'd feed you tiny pots of half and half from McDonald's. Didn't have shit but love for you, Luann.

She stretches out alongside Footer in the bunk. Puzzles things over. There's so much to take in, and all of it is new. She's never thought much about her birthfather, never considered she could have a brother. Breathing strangers fill her ears. Luann can't sleep. She feels Footer's warmth beside her but for the first time remains on her side of the bed.

*

More things disappear. Lockers inside the entrance to Glory Days are busted open. Wallets slip from pockets and purses; watches and rings go missing. One moment a woman is leaning over to snap a photo of her twin four-year-old girls, and the next she cannot find the money she saved for a chicken and gravy dinner, promised souvenirs. During his break Footer holds his arms behind his back, tells Luann to pick a hand—and then presents her with a bracelet of thick gold. Fastens it to her wrist. It's big, and she pushes it up her forearm. Bends over and kisses his cheek. No one has ever given her jewelry.

Happy birthday, sis! he says. She hesitates and then waits for him to explain. Realizes that there are things Footer claims to know that he cannot prove. All these years she has been celebrating her birthday on May 4—who's to say that is correct? She has accepted everything that Teensy and her grandmother have told her, but nothing they have shared has ever made her feel more than inadequate. With Footer she has a story—an extraordinary one.

Footer puts his hand over the bracelet. This belonged to your birthmother, he says, and her heart starts whapping. The questions around her birthmother are never-ending. Why did she give up Luann? How did she end up at St. Mary of the Angels? I didn't know her, he adds, but I knew of her, and here he shakes his head. Makes a clicking sound with his tongue. Your real daddy didn't have a fighting chance with a broad like her. Your birth-mother was the one who done your real daddy wrong. Used him like a tissue. She left in the middle of the night a few weeks after your birth. Went south and west, someplace warm. You weren't enough, Luann. You weren't enough to make her stay.

Luann's mood plummets not only because of what he says but because it is something she has always intuited. Even if Footer is just filling her ears with tales, she begins to understand the hatred she feels for Teensy and her grandmother and this cramped, bland town. Footer, she has begun to see, is her only way out. She decides to remember everything Footer tells her. At least, in doing so, she can distance herself from Ingleside and its small minds. And so she begins to see what he recounts. Heaved on her birthfather's back, an animal hide tied over her for warmth, her birthfather hunts rabbit and squirrel, holds flags of flesh over flames. Afterward the two of them sit on their haunches, suck marrow from bones. She can almost taste the gamy grease, its deep-rooted flavor.

Footer gets her a job making snow cones in the Roaring Twenties section of Glory Days. Here everyone is dressed like flappers or gangsters with bowlers tipped to one side. The streetlights are replica oil lamps, and the cobblestone roads are lined with Model T cutouts.

Luann wears a flapper costume with a beaded headband, a fringed dress. From where she stands squirting colored sugar water on mounds of shaved ice, she can just make out rows of stuffed animals in Footer's booth. When she doesn't have any customers and she looks up, Footer is always watching her.

Be careful around that one, her friend Devin says one night. Devin is dressed in a turquoise polo shirt and white shorts, boat shoes with gold laces. He likes boys, too, and is the closest thing to a best friend Luann has. She wants to know what he means. I've seen him around, is all Devin will say. He's up to no good. She offers him a grape snow cone, and he shakes his head. No thanks.

He knows things about my birthparents, Luann says.

That so, says Devin.

What. What? she asks, squints her eyes at him. Devin checks his watch, says he's got somewhere to be. I'm going to be late, he says, then leans over and kisses her cheeks. She kisses him right back.

The visor of her snow cone stand flutters. Cars tick as they ascend the Tornado, the newest coaster at Glory Days. Overhead a tram carries people from one end of the park to the other, lights a winking trellis. That night, after the gates have closed and the men in jumpsuits get out their brooms and dustpans, the lights at Glory Days flash, but the sound is off, as if the entire park has been muted. Footer won't talk to her. He takes big steps as he heads toward the back of the park. Someone has left a car door open, and music thumps rhythmically like a fist. Fireflies joust beneath a floodlight; quick bodies plink the plastic dome.

She asks Footer what she did wrong—why are you angry? Please tell me, she pleads. Luann catalogs the things she's said, done. She reaches out to Footer before he ascends the steps into the trailer. He flings off her hand. Reaches the top step and whirls around. I saw you kiss that guy, he says, and Luann scans her mind. A shadow casts one side of Footer into darkness, making him appear as if he only has half a face.

Devin? He's just a friend. And he's homosexual.

Footer's mouth opens. He looks at her for a second, snorts a sort of partial smile, and then says, Let's get out of here.

*

Footer says they are getting closer. They're in the woods, walking along the Black River for what has seemed like an hour. He says that her birthfather likes to fish for bluegill and that he throws back everything he catches. He's a real sportsman, your dad. Don't believe in God or any higher power, but every Sunday he is out here like clockwork. Footer makes Luann practice what she will say to him.

Hi, I'm Luann. I'm your daughter.

No. Footer shakes his head. Not like that. You sound like you're selling insurance.

She breathes deep. The damp air reeks of dead animals. Where have you been? she asks, furious. She doesn't know where this anger has been hiding, but it is here now. Why haven't you been looking for me?

There you go, Footer encourages.

You haven't lifted one finger in search of me, she accuses. All this time I've been here—miserable.

That isn't true, says Footer, and then he shoves Luann into the river, thrusts her head beneath the surface, holds it there. She claws sand and rocks, kicks and twists in the brownish yellow murk, and when Footer pulls her up, it is so dark that she can't see his eyes, but she smells him, and she wants to say, what the fuck? But she doesn't. Doesn't say anything. She is too grateful for the clean rush of air.

Don't lie to me, he says. Can't stand liars. He squeezes her arm and then moves away, and in a shaft of moonlight she sees the cuffs of his jeans draw water back like curtains.

Come on, he says. Let's go. She dashes to catch up. The shirt she changed into after work is soaked. Luann squeezes the water out of her hair. She can't find one of her sandals. She thinks it must have floated away, so she takes off the remaining one and holds it. She's pissed off but doesn't say so. Instead, she tells him she's sorry. Only she isn't certain why she's apologizing. Just don't do it again, he says. You can't pull that stuff on me, Luann.

I know you. He charges forward, shakes a finger as he talks. You might be able to pull that crap with other boyfriends but not me.

They walk on, and a tiny niggling inserts itself inside her—go home, it says. *Go.* Only it's too late. Footer has brought her somewhere. Beside the still river, beneath fires that reach into the sky, thirty, forty people party. Someone with a long gray ponytail high-fives Footer. Says, Hey, man! Everyone smiles, laughs. Behind them are mismatched tents arranged without order. Bottles of wine are passed. Someone plays a guitar. Luann stands in front of the fire, shivers. Can't wring any more water out of her clothes.

Why don't you take it all off? asks Footer. Only she's not sure if he's asking or telling. Tries to distill the answer from his expression, but this leaves her equally confused. She wants to remind him a brother wouldn't be such an asshole, except she's too frightened to say or do anything. She tells herself to go along with this charade a little while longer, to give him one more chance. His command is both alluring and frightening. She's never met a man like him.

Footer hands her a can of beer. She lifts to drink it, and he holds the can firm to her lips. She can't drink that fast, and some of it dribbles along the sides of her mouth and down her chest, further dampening her blouse. He must see this but doesn't release the can. When she finishes the beer, he holds up the empty and says: Atta girl! She watches him unbutton her wet blouse, slip it over her shoulders. She's wearing a purple lacy bra, although no one seems to notice.

He puts one arm around her shoulder and walks her around. Everyone knows Footer. Yet he never introduces Luann. She swallows a white pill and drinks every beer offered. Sometimes Footer's hand plays at the back of her bra—gently, playfully. She isn't supposed to touch him. But he can touch her?

Women and men dance naked around the fires. Shadows flicker on their bare skin. When a man with a row of piercings up his ear asks her name, Luann ignores him and then looks to see if Footer has noticed. She doesn't know where he is. Walks around the tents, lingers in front of a rickety picnic table stacked with chips and packages of cookies.

Grows tired of looking. I'll just put my head down for a moment, she thinks, and drifts off. She feels hands all over her, but she can't figure out where they are coming from. Hey little girl, is your daddy home, sings a voice, a familiar one.

*

In the morning, amid white ash and embers, a jumbled mess of sleeping bodies, she cannot find her shirt, can't find Footer either.

Luann hobbles home in her bra and skirt with her one sandal, taking turns wearing it on each foot. By the time she arrives at her grandmother's house, it is nearly noon, and she is sober and starving. Teensy is at the kitchen table when she enters the back door exhausted and shamefaced. He eats a chocolate donut with sprinkles. He must have finished his haul early. Teensy lets her shower and dress before speaking, and then he says real calm, There will be no more of this, staying out all night like some hooligan. You're grounded.

She laughs. His ears flush, his mouth drawn in tight. A week, he adds. And if you don't quit that, it'll soon be two. Your grandmother was worried sick, he adds.

Luann shakes her head. He is so clueless. Does he think Footer is going to agree to this? Teensy's next cross-country assignment is just a day or two away. He isn't going to be here to keep track of her, and her grandmother, with her hearing aid and foods heavy with sausage and salt, isn't any sort of deterrent. It's too late, she thinks. The world Teensy is referring to—the one where she obeys him or even had the chance to do so—has already disappeared.

*

Footer shows her how to make her hand flat, how to slip it inside a pocket quiet and swift. Like a snake striking, he says. And then you've got to get away—don't linger. Move. Jewelry is trickier. Take from the ones who least expect it. They'll give up easy. Footer tells her how one time he took a watch from a retarded man and he started making these honking noises, but since he was retarded, no one thought it unusual.

Meanwhile, there are sirens. Police canvass the park, batons in hand. The *Ingleside Courier* runs a special edition on personal safety. They remind readers to lock their doors and carry a limited amount of cash. But they don't understand Footer. He cannot be stopped. Whatever Footer wants, he will take. And everything, according to Footer, is worth taking. Luann has long considered herself a mostly good girl, but she feels herself being absorbed by Footer and his wants. There is no room for pause. Her life might as well belong to him.

Luann selects an older bowlegged couple for her first theft. She watches them exit the park at dusk. They walk hand in hand and wonder aloud where they parked their car. Luann darts forward and yanks the woman's purse off her elbow. Old broad hangs on and falls down in a quiet crumble, yet she does not release the bag. The old man tells the woman to give Luann her purse.

She's got a gun, Louise!

Luann does not have a gun. Shame on you, the woman says, and in the energy required by this utterance, Luann seizes the bag and runs off. The woman screams, Help, police!

Her rheumy eyes look just like Luann's grandmother, and so it feels good to pretend she is taking from this bitter woman, someone who has never hid her disdain for Luann, for how she came to be.

July bleeds on. Despite the thefts, crowds at Glory Days swell. Luann heads through the Colonial Times section of the park, past the Yankee Clipper water ride and Ye Olde Time Photography Studio, where you can dress in period clothes and have a sepia-tinged photo taken in a covered wagon. She takes her place at her stand and starts filling cups with ice. Halfway into her shift a missing child's name is announced on loudspeaker. An hour passes, then two. They lock down the park.

She makes small talk with Footer over a late-afternoon order of chili fries under one of the red-and-white umbrellas. You hear about that kid?

Kids get lost all the time, he says distractedly. But Footer seems odd. His head. How he hoards it.

You feeling okay? she asks. He does not answer except to ask about her efforts that day. When she hands him the contents of a man's slender billfold, he snorts.

Seriously? You want to be stuck here your whole life? I thought you wanted to meet your birthfather and get out of this dump. He smacks the back of her head, calls her a fool. Tears clot her eyes, and if she were braver, she would stand up and run. But where can she go?

Footer waves the bills. This stuff doesn't grow on trees, Luann. I know.

I know, he mocks with a forced falsetto. I know I know I know. I'm tired of the lip service.

I'll try harder, she says.

Damn right you will. Come on. I want to show you something. He takes her to a building out back where they keep the tools and cleaning supplies. There, inside one of the lockers, she sees him—knows who he is before Footer says a thing. The missing boy. He is red-faced, and his skin is shiny with sweat and tears. His cheeks are pressed up against the grates. Mommy! He cries. Mommy!

Just like a pet raccoon, Footer says, squiggling a finger between the grates, his expression suddenly bright. The boy screams, and Footer slams a fist into the locker beside where the boy is stuffed. He momentarily silences. Chili fries flood Luann's mouth, and she has to push open the metal door and get out. Vomit splats the asphalt in an orange flash.

I always let them go, Footer says, following her. I just take them for a little bit. Wait till you see how much those kids are savored afterward. Maybe they'd value you more if you went away for a bit. Ever consider that?

*

Men in navy caps with walkie-talkies search the park, stand at attention near the Tornado and the Torpedo. Luann hasn't forgotten the sound of the first boy screaming for his mommy between the shelves of disinfectant and liquid soap, so after three weeks, when there is another kidnapping, Luann considers running to the building with the lockers. This time a boy has disappeared from the Kiddie Koaster, a dragon-themed ride that chugs an oblong track. Luann wonders if there is some way to make it seem like the boy has escaped. The park goes on lockdown, and the line for her stand stretches to a candy shop known for its fudge. They aren't letting anyone out of the park, so everyone is either eating or shopping.

After another announcement for the missing boy, Luann ditches her booth and rushes to the lockers. There is no one there. Soon after she learns that the missing boy has appeared in the food court, and she hurries over, spies him sucking on a cherry Slurpee. There is a bruise over his eye that has become a small hive. The boy's mother crouches on her bare knees, sobs as they're reunited. Security flanks the mother, helps her stand. He's a strong little bugger, Footer later says, shows Luann the bite marks on his arm. Had to teach him a lesson.

And then he's gone. Two, three days pass, and no Footer. An older bald guy takes his place at the Gangster Shootout. Three tries for a dollar, he sings. When Luann asks about Footer, the guy shrugs. *Want a try? It's on the house*, his grin wet.

Luann should be relieved, yet she doesn't trust his disappearance. She knows Footer watches her. She feels his presence in the sticky sweat that trickles down her armpits and the backs of her knees. Luann looks for Footer in the park and on her way to and from work. School will start up again in a few weeks, and the whole notion of it makes her sleepy. After this summer how could she think of sitting at a desk?

The longer Footer is gone, the more she begins to think that maybe he really has moved on. At night, after her shift ends, a group meets at Katy's Place. Luann isn't legal age, but that doesn't matter. She sips beer fat with foam. Taps her foot to music. A college guy buys her a drink. Pulls her on the dance floor, whispers in her ear. What are you, nineteen?

He licks a finger, runs it along her collarbone. Jailbait. That's what you are.

She laughs. Inside her denim skirt her legs are shaved. Seventeen years old, and Luann can do as she pleases. It's been more than two weeks, and the more she drinks, the stronger the sense grows: No guy is going to tell her what to do. She doesn't need Footer or anyone else for that matter. She lets the college guy twirl her around the floor, his hand tucked in the back pocket of her skirt. She tries to keep track of the drinks he buys, what she'll later owe him.

*

It's late, and she is in her bed drifting off to sleep when Teensy enters her room. She jumps a bit, never has been able to keep track of his schedule. The fixture from the hall spills into her bedroom. I don't know what you've been up to, Luann, but you've got to quit it, he says. I won't have you living in this house like this—coming and going at all hours. Driving your grandmother and me sick.

She fingers sleep from her eyes, pushes up on her elbows. Her mouth tastes funny.

His eyes are such a clear blue. At this early-morning hour it seems she's forgotten what he really looks like. Teensy clears his throat. I don't know what you want from me. I've done the best I can, Luann. Trying to pay the bills and put money aside for your future. I want to give you a life better than the one your mother or I ever had. Is that so wrong? She can see him shaking his head. You seem dead set on destroying everything I'm trying to create.

Luann trembles with rage. I know about my birthparents, she spurts. I know about the hunting cabin, my mama birthing me in the river. I know she left.

He stands there. Rubs his eyelids with his thumbs, and when he takes his hands away, it looks like he's been punched. Don't quite know what to say. You can believe whatever you want, but the only thing that matters is the night that nun called and we went to Chicago and they placed you in your mother's arms. The two of us had never been happier. That's the god-honest truth.

She continues. I know about the snow, the duct tape—how my birthfather snuck into McDonald's and fed me creamer. She waits for some flicker to appear on his face. You've never told me anything. You've just kept it all to yourself as if it might go away.

You can believe anything you want, Luann. Doesn't mean that it's true. But I won't have you living under my roof like some derelict. She snorts. When he shuts the door, she does not realize this is good-bye. She reconfigures the blankets. Closes her eyes. Sleeps.

This time a memory of her own surfaces in a dream. Her birthfather has caked her face with dirt and shredded her clothes. He has removed her shoes even though it's November and the chill pavement pricks her feet. Hands pork colored, she stands outside a diner with a can. She can't be more than three or four years old. Her father is ill. He has stomach cramps so bad that he can't stand upright—everything runs out of him. She raises the can every time the diner door opens. Please help, she says. Everything is cloudy and smudged. Luann wonders if her birthfather has put mud in her eyes. The brightness dims further, her throat tightens, air constricts. She's chilled, and her father is a brown mess inside their tent. It's suddenly hard to breathe, to take in air. Her lungs burn, and her eyes fling open; Luann gasps when she sees Footer standing over her, hands at her throat, the memory extinguished.

I could kill you, he says, tightening his grip. Stupid broad. What makes you think you're worth keeping alive?

She kicks and kicks, and the bed shakes. She sinks into it, the impossibility of escape and her long-standing stupidity. When she is about wrung out, he lets go.

Luann sees stars. Everything tingles. She runs a hand at her neck real slow.

Why did you have to do me wrong? Why, Luann? He shakes his head at her. She can only make squeaks. Keeps touching her neck. It's futile, don't you see? I am everything now. The wind in the branches, cat face of an oak, deer flushing a hill. I'm in the old woman's snores, her wet gasps for air. I'm the silt between your legs as you think of me, hoping for anything better than what you've had before—the ache in your heart, what you know to be untrue. I know you, Luann. I've always known you.

He tells her to dress, says they're going for a drive. She pulls off the oversized T-shirt she wears, and Footer smiles at her nakedness. She goes to the dresser, selects her warmest sweater, then follows Footer downstairs. She sees Teensy asleep on the couch. Tomorrow he will drive his trailer to Wyoming or Montana or some other western state. It will be days before he learns she is gone.

She shivers in the car, and Footer turns the heat on high, then lights a cigarette, rolls down the window. Luann thinks about her birthfather as they drive. He doesn't know what the kids at school say about her, hasn't seen her report cards. Her birthfather will be happy to know she is alive, to discover she shares half his genes. She imagines meeting him will be like starting over. She'll wear less makeup. Change her jeans more frequently. Maybe begin reading books. She wants to be a good daughter. Knows in her heart the potential exists. She doesn't ask Footer where they are going. She keeps the questions to herself. Still, Luann wonders: How long will it take, and will her birthfather still be there; is she worth the wait?

SURROUNDED

LUANN HEARS THE SIRENS SLIPPING OFF THE TREES, thin-necked siphons that can't hold tight to any sound, and she moves away from the window by the sink. Hope that she's been kindling runs free, and she lets it. Doesn't tap it down. Luann sees everything clear up inside her head. She feels the police cars jostle over the bridge and accelerate to make the rise toward the abandoned hunting cabin where she and Footer have been living the better part of the past year. Farther out is that empty expanse of land that, if you look real close, still stabbed of corn. Just beyond is the hill where Footer took the boy—Jeremiah.

It's late morning, and Glory Days is only open half-days now that school is back in session. If Luann listens hard, she can hear them running tests on the rides. They let the coasters pass by with empty cars to smooth the dew on the track and clear it of nighttime debris. Both she and Footer are supposed to work that afternoon, she thinks, but she knows they won't be going.

The scavenger hunt had been Footer's idea, but Jeremiah would have screamed or made some ruckus if she hadn't nodded and gave him a small wink when she transferred the boy's hand from hers to Footer's. She watched them take to the hill, scramble up the incline, their feet slip-slopping on old leaves and broken branches. Jeremiah twisted to look at Luann one last time. His eyes were the color of walnuts.

On the TV his mother says Jeremiah likes Matchbox cars and dreams of becoming a firefighter like his uncle. His father says they'd just like their little boy to come home. But this, Luann thinks, is an impossibility.

For some time Luann and Footer had been snatching kids from the park. They never meant much harm. They only took them away for a few hours. Footer would be all hopped up in advance, explaining how what they were doing would make the world a better place. *It's a small world after all, it's a small world,* he sang, hands twisted in a heap below his chin.

"Think how happy folks will be to get them back. Think of them hugs, Luann. The biggest hug you ever imagined. Afterward these kids are gonna be savored like pumpkin pie on the Thanksgiving table."

In those days Luann was easily persuaded. So they made a commotion near the kiddie ride, then skirted a child away. They hung out in one of the old storage areas at the back of the park for a few hours and gave a kid all the suckers he wanted, then stuffed him in a locker. Most of them were too frightened to do anything but cry. But Jeremiah was different. He bit Footer when he hoisted him up into the locker. And then Footer tossed him against a rack of empty shelves. Jeremiah fell into a jumbled heap, and it reminded Luann of that one time, the time years before now—arms and legs knocking inside her at night—how she could cup the bend of a foot or trace the outline of an elbow beneath the skin of her stomach.

Luann rushed to Jeremiah, scooped him onto her lap, and rocked him. He didn't cry. He wore a dazed expression. "Come on!" Footer motioned excitedly for the door. Jeremiah had broken the skin on Footer's hand, and Footer put that part of himself in his mouth to suck the trickle of blood. "We're going on a scavenger hunt." This was news to Luann, but she knew better than to question Footer. She helped the boy stand and took his hand.

Luann wishes things had gone differently. She didn't say anything to Footer when he came back from the other side of the hill alone. He would just give her something to dull her nerves. But the boy. Jeremiah. What they did was a mistake.

*

Inside the cabin Luann smells the earth's fallowness. Though the cows are long gone and nobody makes a living off the land anymore, fall once meant work. She knows her dad, Teensy, would be aware of the same thing. This time of year the cows needed to be weighed, each one stuffed inside the squeeze chute where they poured over the parasite control, vaccinated the calves, and pregnancy-checked the heifers. And when her legs were about to fall off from exhaustion, they would sample the soil and then frost seed the clover.

Luann and Teensy are not speaking again, although the hunting cabin where she and Footer live is a mile from Teensy's house. Her grandmother has been gone nearly two years now, and their cows were long ago sold off, but the ground remains rutted. The last time Luann saw Teensy, he stood at the door of the cabin with two plastic grocery bags bulging with canned vegetables and crackers, and when she spotted the rind of an orange, she nearly wept. Footer had shoved her aside and spoke all cheery, taking the bags, "Welcome, Teensy!" Luann's stomach was pronounced then, and Teensy's gaze moved right through her and settled on it. He stood there holding his cap, shifting his weight from one foot to the other while Footer unpacked the groceries. Footer jabbered on in his way, and when he left to get wood for the stove, Teensy fixated on her stomach and asked her what she was going do.

"Don't matter. Footer says there's no heartbeat."

"Have you been to a doctor?" Teensy asked.

"Haven't had time," she mumbled. Turned a can of pork and beans in her hands just to have something to do.

"I could take care of it," he said. "I'd do just fine. Know I would."

She shook her head. "Can't care for something that isn't alive just because you wish it to be."

"Let me take you to the doctor in Streatmore," he said. "No one needs to know." And before she knew what was happening, Teensy crouched down, turned his face to the side, and pressed it against her stomach. She tried to push him away, but he held her hips. She couldn't recall the last time she'd been touched by him, and she felt both drawn to his familiarity and frayed by the ghosts those hands had touched.

"Leave off!" she yelled, not altogether meaning it.

Footer came in then, his arms full of wood. He dropped the load and told Teensy to let her go. He shook him by his shoulders like a sack of meal. "Get out of here, man. Just go."

In between then and now there has been lots of time to think about what might have been if she'd let Teensy take her to Streatmore or follow him down some new road away from here. Seeing part of her alive in someone else. Anything would have been worth that.

She regrets all of it. Can think clearly enough to say it. She hates Footer for making her give her boy away like a pair of overused shoes. Luann hates Footer's pills and excuses and can't even stand the warped way he speaks. They were all lies. Everything from his mouth is a lie. At one point those falsehoods kept her going. Made her feel special. That time had long passed.

The sirens are more distinct now, and Luann splits the blinds, peers out, and then Footer comes up out of nowhere and slaps her hand away. "You want to announce to the world we're here? We're gonna stay put, wait for it to blow over. They don't know nothing. Just got to wait them out." He squeezes her chin, kisses her mouth. She doesn't feel anything. He pours cereal into a bowl, but they are out of milk, so he uses water from the tap. His hands tremble as he lifts the spoon. Not yet noon, and he already has that jittery look.

Footer's eyes skate back and forth beneath heavy brows. He holds the bowl close to his mouth, scoops cereal faster. He misses, and a flake sticks to his cheek, another sops to the floor. Luann turns, takes the few steps to the room where they slept. Still needs to dress. Her heart beats fast, but her mind has a blank calmness to it. She strips off her bedclothes and looks at herself in a bit of mirror she found in a dresser drawer. She traces the line that cuts across the top of her underwear. She has lost the desire to eat, but her belly remains gummy soft. The extra pouch of skin at her middle is gathered like a drawstring purse. Somewhere there is a boy. Her son. He doesn't know anything about Luann. She is just a name on a piece of paper. Luann grazes the scar. It is a comfort to have it right there.

Luann puts on clean underwear and jeans, a shirt that covers her elbows. She feels better once most of her skin is secreted. In the bathroom she squeezes the rest of the toothpaste onto her brush and cleans her mouth as if it's any other day. The sirens fill the cabin, but the sun is so bright behind the drawn blinds that she can't see the flashing lights even though she knows they're coming. Just like she knew the abducted boy's name was Jeremiah and that he had a spate of freckles across his cheeks and nose. Fair skinned and redheaded, he had a younger sister, and in all the televised conferences she held a rag doll, the kind that's pillow soft with yarn hair and painted-on features. The kind you don't see much anymore. Footer makes her turn it off if Jeremiah's family comes on TV. "Why you watching that junk, Luann? It's not good for you. You know that."

Then he'd tell her to come over to where he lounged, and he'd motion with a hand for her to turn around. Sometimes he'd have her lift her shirt and push her bra up, ask for her to bounce like a cheerleader and make them jiggle. It always brought a goofy smile to his face. He'd give her a sloppy kiss, something that made a smacking sound and left a wet spot. Soon after he'd pass out with a little grin on his face. But while he slept it off, she turned the tube back on, dragged a chair in front of the screen, and stared at photos of Jeremiah's parents, his sister. The puffed, slacken look of his mother's face. Luann feels the scar rub up against the band of her jeans, and she knows she wears the same stricken look. Even though it has been more than a year, she knows she'll wear that look the rest of her life.

*

Footer sits at the table in front of the toaster trimming his eyebrows with a pair of toenail clippers. The sirens are so loud, the place nearly shudders. They are parked outside, she is sure of it. Her throat goes dry, hands and armpits sweaty.

Luann had been the one to make the call to the police at the MiniMart pay phone. She hiked out in the earliest of hours that morning beneath a cavern of stars; leaves crunched underfoot, nothing but blackness all around her, the river low but its stench rich. Everything was drying, dropping, fading away. She wasn't used to being alone at that hour in the woods, and it flared up in her a remembering for how the thistle and alfalfa would go gray with the first frost. Heads on the clover would shrivel and droop, but in the morning steam would rise from the ground, and the breath of each cow would be visible. In autumn Teensy would shake her awake before dawn. Sometimes he would place a hand on her shoulder; other times he'd stand in the doorway for a few moments before calling her name, saying it was time to get up and that there was work to do.

Truth is she woke as soon as he opened the door to her room and just kept quiet. Luann never saw Teensy's face during these moments, but she knew he was memorizing her. Just thinking about it again makes her want to run home to Teensy and bury her head in his arms and apologize. Tell him what she has yet to speak of—the bright hospital lights raining down, blinding her, the rip-roaring pain of each contraction—how the nurses held her firm, shot her looks of disgust. They'd given her something to deaden everything below her waist, but she'd still felt some tugging and turning as they pulled him from her body. His cry boomed off the tiled walls, and the pureness of that sound made everything shimmer. And then they'd whisked him away. For weeks afterward her breasts wept with milk whether or not she thought of him.

The car doors open, footsteps are on the porch. She places a hand on the wall. Luann glimpses shadows on the other side of the blinds and braces herself.

GLORY DAYS

JEREMIAH IS IN A PLACE HE KNOWS WELL. The close-cropped smell of the log ride, the exhaust from the old-time cars, the spooky sounds playing on the loudspeaker as the cars ascend the track—it's Halloween weekend at Glory Days, once his favorite time. Jeremiah lifts up, flies from ground level to the elevation of a bird perched in the trees. He straddles an oblong-shaped fixture that looks like a rocket outside the chamber of Fredonia the Great in the Futurama section of the park. Jeremiah has come here nearly every day in the past eleven months. Though he's only ten years old, he can see more than any person alive.

The days are short, the nights cool. It hasn't rained for weeks, and the river is as thick and unmoving as cake batter. Carp wash up on the banks. Jeremiah knows that if he were still alive, he would spend his days poking their sticky, motionless bodies with the end of a stick. But first he would explore the shore in search of the ones whose gills continued to flap, and then he'd push these fish back into the river, wait to see if waves trickled the surface or if their bodies floated up.

Or maybe he'd use his pocketknife to gut the biggest fish, its insides slithering out onto the shore, wet and lifeless. Like what the man had almost done to Jeremiah when he killed him. And then he saw it all over again. He didn't like to recall it—didn't like it one bit, but once the recollection started, Jeremiah could not stop it.

He felt his hand inside Footer's as they climbed the hill. Footer had promised him a dollar if he found a snake nest, but once they got to the top, Jeremiah only noticed a deep hole, and then he was seized by a great pain on the side of his head. When he woke, he felt the dirt clenching his nostrils and lurching down his throat. He was somewhere in the barren limbs of a dead elm, and he was looking down at himself. His clothes were off and heaped to the side, and his body was inside the hole.

Now he notices all kinds of things. His mama's weeping, his daddy twisting the band he wears on his left hand. Jeremiah looks from here to there in an instant, and it's like watching TV with the world's fastest remote control. The other kids say it's not good for him to see so much. You've got to train your eyes to look elsewhere, they say. They're older than him and have been here longer, so he nods and acts like he's listening, but all the while he's thinking about the fact that Fredonia the Great knows he's there. His hope for release from this in-between place resides with her.

One of the most popular attractions at Glory Days, Fredonia the Great receives visions of how a person will die. Jeremiah wants to tell her everything: His mama closed the door to his room with its unmade bed, and Lego pieces still scatter the floor. Although it's been close to a year, she still sobs out of nowhere, and then his daddy pulls her close, while Buster barks at the neighbor's cat. His sister has nightmares and wakes screaming most nights. Jeremiah's head aches, but he doesn't know what to do with all these images. He is dead. He shouldn't be able to see any of it.

Below, Jeremiah sees his fourth-grade classmates waving glow sticks, free tonight for anyone with paid admission. He imagines himself ringing doorbells until his pillowcase is filled with treats, porch lights go out, and people quit answering their doors.

It wouldn't be like that for him, not this year, not ever.

Jeremiah zooms down to the line of people waiting to see Fredonia the Great. He bends over and ties together the shoelaces of a preschooler standing between his parents. The preschooler takes a step, falls over, lifts his face, and begins to cry. Jeremiah points and laughs at him. Sucker! he says. He knows it's not kind, but he is changing. Already he detects all the goodness leaving him. Inside, black thoughts have begun to burble. It isn't fair that his classmates get to go trick-or-treating; it isn't fair that they can play with their toys or sleep in beds with blankets. If they are suddenly woken in the middle of the night, they can walk down the hall to their parents' bedroom, slip between their sleeping bodies.

Jeremiah remembers how as a youngster his mother used to scoop him onto her lap when he first woke. She would rock him, call him her sweet boy, but even this recollection, this tenderness, has begun to fade.

*

At first Fredonia the Great thinks the spirit is a dream, some wrecked possibility. For decades she has offered visions to the people of Ingleside, and now she offers this to paying visitors of Glory Days. But no, that isn't it. This is different. Someone or something lingers.

Fredonia the Great senses that there is a message this spirit is trying to relay, but she doesn't understand it. Leave me alone, she thinks. She feels the eyes of the patrons waiting in line for their visions. They think it is a feat to be the oldest woman in town. *I would like to live forever*, a teenage girl told her the week prior, and Fredonia the Great had been so jolted by this admission that she didn't have a response. There is nothing in this town, in this life, for Fredonia the Great.

As she stretches in her own bed at night, decades of visions return in suffocating wholeness. The images come fast, and Fredonia feels each one all over again—a man falls from a building; a woman with ankles and wrists as thick as sausages bleeds in her bed, a baby forever motionless in the pooch of her stomach. A little boy turns blue, his lips puckered around a pebble. Fredonia recalls the sound of the balers, dust rising up from the till. Back then Ingleside had dirt roads and banks of trees and always the river with its green fertile scent. She wakes with a start and remembers all over again that the fields have sprouted new weekend homes, and not too far away stores that are as big as football fields stretch out where corn tassels once swayed. Still, it is hard to look and not see the farms cowering. Now there's the chatter of rides on their tracks, screams clinging to wind.

Fredonia the Great feels nothing for the strangers with their athletic shoes and fanny packs waiting in line two or three hours, faces blank as churches. Go on, she says, patting the velvet-covered bed for an elderly man with a walker. His friend helps him up. The lights are muted. He smells of hot dogs and the metal handrails that mark the perimeter of rides. She instructs him to keep his arms at his sides.

She closes his eyelids. Places her hands on his chest, and her mind flashes back in the familiar blush of a vision. She sees him cower in a hospital bed surrounded by family—his children and grandchildren. Fredonia speaks of the figures that appear. *They are holding hands, saying prayers, telling you they love you. You're not far off*, she says, and when she finishes, he looks at her and says thank you.

You're welcome, she says, as the next person hovers and the line snakes around the building.

Fredonia the Great watches the man move toward the exit, his low-hunched walk. He can't be much younger than her. To be so fortunate, she thinks. If she had the power to do so, she would lie down now and take her last breath. Fredonia the Great's daughter won't speak to her, and she hasn't seen her grandson in many years, and after that what else matters? Her husband has now been deceased longer than he was alive. She'd like nothing better than to turn to the ground of her undoing.

Instead, there is the spirit. It hangs onto her skirt or lingers along the gold-sprayed throne of her chamber. It hesitates so close at times that she's developed an idea of its size. She doesn't hear chimes trickling the air or windows opening of their own accord. She doesn't know what he wants from her, and now she must face the fact that even the dead will not leave her alone. I can't help you! she'd like to say, or leave me alone! But it is no use. The spirit follows her, trails her from place to place. It's all fun and games to you, she thinks. I've got a job to do. Let me suffer this day in peace.

She eats a handful of almonds, sips tea that cooled long ago. The sound of a witch cackles over the loudspeaker outside, mixes with laughter and faraway screams from the Tornado, the park's famed coaster. The moon shifts high. There is no time for a break.

*

Jeremiah asks the other spirits how long they've been here, and they shrug. It doesn't matter. Forever? one tries, and Jeremiah feels his insides lurch. They say if he can get out of here, he won't have to see it anymore and then he can forget Footer's face, his graveled voice. But no one can tell him what he needs to do to move on. The other kids don't seem to mind watching life go on without them, and unlike Jeremiah, they don't seem haunted by how they arrived at this in-between place. There is no one to force them to eat peas or take showers. Plus, they can fly! Nobody tells them what they can or cannot do, but as the months wear on, these are the very things Jeremiah misses.

He returns to the tiny tan house with the crooked shutters. The gutters stuffed with last fall's leaves. Inside his room he spots his half-finished ship and unmade bed, blankets bunched and battered just like he left them, a pile of dirty socks. His favorite shirt, the one that has a Tyrannosaurus Rex on the front with its tail extending down one arm, straddles a chair. Jeremiah pretends that he's skipped school or, better yet, that he's home sick and his mom has taken off work and is in the other room making him hot cocoa and toast. He nestles in his blankets. Turns his face to the side, lets out a great yawn. His sister refuses to sleep in her room, so they've made a bed from an old air mattress on the floor beside where his parents sleep. Jeremiah was certain he could sleep anywhere if he had the chance. With a little rest everything would improve.

Footsteps crunch leaves on the sidewalk, and the doorbell keeps ringing, only there is no one home. Trick or treat! the voices call—children just like him. They tear into packages of M&Ms and make fart sounds with their armpits. He stuffs his pillow over his head, but the noise continues.

Last Halloween Jeremiah had planned to dress as a storm trooper from Star Wars. He picked out his costume at the Super Saver, and they'd placed it on layaway. His mama put down five dollars on it every Saturday before his death. Now his costume hangs in a plastic bag in the back of her closet, and seeing it there like some lifeless body makes Jeremiah's face go hot. The feeling rises up in him clear and insistent. He doesn't want to be here! He storms into the kitchen, grabs a pack of matches from the junk drawer, and stuffs them into his pocket.

He flies fast, high into the air above Glory Days, and returns to the booth of Fredonia the Great. She leans over a guest, guides her onto the bed. Jeremiah pushes with all his might on the woman's bottom half until she spills over onto the ground. Jeremiah hops up in her place, points and laughs at the fallen woman. Her eyes go wide as she looks around. *I'm sorry,* Fredonia stammers. *So sorry.*

What happened? the woman asks.

Fredonia brushes the question away with her hand as she helps the woman up, then turns and looks in Jeremiah's direction.

Jeremiah reaches for Fredonia. You've got to help me, he says to her, grasping her face in his hands. He has never touched Fredonia like this, and he is surprised by how pliable her skin feels. He holds her jaw and tightens his grip, watches her swallow. Her eyes dart to the patrons in line, and Jeremiah thinks how pleasant it is to hold a living thing in his hands. I don't want to be here, he says.

She sees him, he is certain of it, and then she wrenches herself away, turns to the next waiting person, and places her hands on them as they stand. Jeremiah's face grows hot. I'm talking to you! He yells and jumps off the bed, grabs Fredonia the Great at the waist. He tries to sit her down. Why is she still alive while Jeremiah is dead and stuck in this forsaken place? No more Mr. Nice Guy, he thinks. But Fredonia the Great surprises him. Her left leg jousts from her skirt, smacks Jeremiah's gut, and sends him sailing into a corner.

As he slumps there, it comes back stronger than ever. He hears things crunching under his gym shoes. The woman with the soft voice had been there too. Luann. He has not forgotten her name. And then he feels the chapped clamminess of the man's palm, and all of it makes his insides twist, and he thinks he might be sick, but that can't be. He's lost the ability to vomit. You aren't alive, dodo, he thinks, and it's your own stupid fault.

He holds his head and tries to squeeze the memory away, but it won't stop.

We'll play the game for a little while, Luann had said, squeezing his shoulder and walking him a ways behind a den of trees before taking his hand and depositing it inside Footer's. He went along as complacent as a peach. Why didn't he yell and kick and scream?

Jeremiah leaves Fredonia the Great's chamber for the roof of the Hay Baler just a few rides away. It's cold, and his nose runs. It dribbles into the top of his shirt. There's no Kleenex, and his eyes fill up, and then hot tears slide down his cheeks. No one notices that Jeremiah is crying outside in the cold. He swipes at his face. Fog rises from a machine they've hidden behind a casket that opens and closes. As he shivers, the smoke lifts up, and he takes out the matches. Heavy metal music blares from below. He knows what he must do.

There is a bell inside a little house on top of the Hay Baler ride where the birds have left a nest. It is here that Jeremiah strikes a match. It ignites quickly, a tiny trickle of smoke. He warms his hands, mesmerized by the new glow. It flickers and wavers, grows. Snaps up the gray soft stuff the birds have used to line their bed.

He sits cross-legged and marvels at the warmth, rubs his hands in slow circles. This feels good. He wishes his parents could see him and this fire of his own making. Jeremiah is growing up! He isn't a baby. He can fly and see things others cannot. He pictures his dad putting an arm around his shoulders. There you go, bud! That's right! My little man.

Jeremiah is deep in his thoughts when the bell for the ride goes off; the piercing sound rattles with intensity, and his leg kicks the fire. When he rights himself, he can see that the fire has changed. It's wider now, squat, and he has to back up, give it room.

Yet he is grateful for the warmth. Now he can think. The nest is gone, and the fire has grown. He scoots back farther and sees how the flames surround the bell.

He hears laughter and screaming below. Maybe someone is hurt. Jeremiah is a bad, bad boy. He feels the whir of the ride spinning beneath him; cracks leak air, float up to him like whispers. Everything is warm and toasty. He can see a giant cheeseburger spinning on its plate outside the diner in the Fabulous Fifties section. Inside the waitresses wear poodle skirts, deliver milkshakes piled high with whipped cream and cherries. His dad took him there sometimes when he was in a good mood. They'd sit at the counter and order their food, and Jeremiah would flip through the jukebox. The music they played there was different. None of it familiar. The voices were higher and the melodies sweet. It wasn't like the heavy metal that reverberated from the Hay Baler ride or in the background of the games in the Roaring Twenties section of the park. This is the kind of music they played when I was a boy, his dad had said once, years ago. And that day was the first time Jeremiah had considered it: his dad had once been a kid. He remembered feeling weird inside, a nugget of his bun lodging in his throat. What about me, Jeremiah had asked.

You? Well you weren't here then.

It made him feel sad all over again to think about it. The fries hadn't tasted good after that, and Jeremiah let them congeal in a pile on his plate.

He realizes he's hot and wipes perspiration from his face and neck. Jeremiah stands, and the night air instantly chills. The fire is large, much too large to keep him warm. He wishes some of the older kids were with him. They could have their own Halloween bonfire right here, thanks to Jeremiah. The fire snaps and pops, embers shoot into the sky. Below sirens wail, and there is shouting. From where he stands, he can see Fredonia the Great's booth.

A girl his own age joins him on the roof of the Hay Baler. Did you do this? she asks. He shrugs. Jeremiah isn't going to admit anything. His days being obedient are over.

*

At first Fredonia the Great thinks it's just part of the evening show. There are fireworks most nights, but she doesn't usually notice them from her chamber. The brightness beyond the window beckons like a rising sun. Black smoke unravels, heads and necks crane, and a low murmur has begun to rise from the guests in line. There is a sudden flash, and people take off running and screaming from her chamber. Outside on the cobblestone streets hundreds of people push and yell, while a recording on the overhead speaker thanks guests for visiting, then instructs them to exit the park at once and have a Glory Day!

The smoke chokes the air with a heavy chemical smell. Fredonia the Great faces the window, sees flames stretch like arms from the roof of the Hay Baler ride just down the street. The fixtures in her chamber begin to flicker, and the last remaining guests shove out the doors. Fredonia watches the flames, mesmerized. The screams tear the night air, but she is calmed by her closeness to this destruction. This is it, she thinks. Recognizes her end. She feels herself moving closer to her beloved, her parents and the grandmother who had first taught her how to be a healer. Yes, she thinks, shedding her turban on the floor of her chamber, yes.

The firefighters hose the thing with water, but it doesn't make a bit of difference. As they swing their axes at the flimsy walls, part of the roof of the ride crashes in, forces up a blast of smoke and ash. The firefighters redirect the spray and hook up another hose. They use their hatchets to open a wall that's not yet on fire as Fredonia the Great moves toward the flames. *Lady, give us room*, they say. But she's not listening. Fredonia the Great pushes forward until someone grabs her shoulders. *You can't go in there, lady. Are you crazy?* He holds her steady though she squirms, and then another wall crumbles, and everyone scrambles. There are people in there, she says. I can help.

Everyone move out, it's gonna blow, someone yells, and here she is released. Fredonia the Great darts toward the ride and drops to her knees. She crawls inside the entrance, feels her way across the floor of the Hay Baler on hands and knees. Every wall is on fire, but somehow she knows which direction to travel. *Help me!* the voices scream, and she sees them in her mind—six or seven of them; they've tipped the cars of the ride on their sides and huddle together wailing and yelling for help. She turns away from the yelling and screaming and plants herself beside a wall of fire. She waits for the flames to arrive. It will hurt momentarily, she understands, but the end—this is a gift.

Suddenly, the spirit's presence is palpable. She should help them, is that what it's trying to tell her? And then she knows. This is it, she thinks, her chance to save the living.

She tries to find them—turns toward their screams. I'm coming, she says. Stay put! Only the smoke is thick and gritty. It makes her head go dotty. Her slipper shoe pokes the track, and the metal is hot to the touch. She crawls sideways, heads in the direction of the voices but encounters a wall of fire.

The heat wafts from somewhere else, and she is surprised by how vast this place seems. It comes to her in a rush: All her years at Glory Days, and she never once boarded a ride. She never fixed straps over her shoulders so she could be thrown into the sky only to hurtle down in safety. Despite the brilliance of the fire, everything she sees grows hazy. Where are you? she calls, wills herself forward, tries to call up an idea of where these guests might be.

We'll get you out of here, she thinks. Don't worry. Their safety depends on her. There are sirens and screams, and the bitter taste in Fredonia's mouth suffocates. Visions storm inside her. They sweep her over.

REMAINS

WE GATHER OUTSIDE GLORY DAYS and lace our fingers in the fence. The quiet is an ache we feel. Leaves bat our legs, and carrion birds pace the sky. Some of us are dressed in the knit shirts we wear while pushing brooms or working concessions, ringing up trinkets in the gift shop. Go home, a man in a suit tells us. Go home to your families.

And do what? we ask. What can we do now?

The funeral procession snakes through downtown Ingleside. The cemetery is full of cars; the smell of lilies and honeysuckle slick the air. Already there are rumors that it won't reopen. That the state might shut it down for good. The exits, we hear. Should have been more exits.

None of us are supposed to be here. They closed the amusement park immediately after. The sky was blanketed with clouds, and an angry stench choked our clothes, made our eyes sting. But it doesn't feel right to stand here and peer in. So we wait until the men in suits get into their shiny black cars, and then we let ourselves in through a gap someone cut in the fence. Yellow ribbons flap. They've already bulldozed it, and now our shoes crunch rubble. There were six of them. By the time the firefighters reached them, it was too late.

We walk the perimeter of the Hay Baler and fix our eyes downward. In the remains we discover a mother's leather purse, a man's wristwatch, the melted remains of a toy bunny. We push ash aside with our shoes, drop to our knees, and dig. It doesn't need to be large. There is only rubble, grainy bits that color our hands gray. We work in silence, make our hands trowels, clear cinder.

Earlier today the men stood before the microphones, said nothing like this had ever happened before. The photographers captured them placing bouquets of flowers and stuffed animals in front of the entrance to Glory Days.

Our memories are different. We saw them making out behind the midway. We watched them eat buckets of caramel corn and shoehorns of cotton candy. They chewed with their mouths open, their fingers sticky. They gazed past us—didn't glance at our name tags or ask what it was like to be from here, to grow up in Ingleside. Still, we checked to make sure the lap belt was on tight, reached to secure the harness, our fingers bumping their hips or chests. They never flinched, and it was as if we weren't even there.

We swept the grounds, emptied trash bins, picked up wads of chewed gum. We sold them cheap necklaces and sweaty Cokes and, when it rained, ponchos. When their kids got lost, we stayed with them, gave them coloring books and juice boxes. Waited for them to be claimed. All these years, and we never knew them. Didn't realize their bodies could burn or that it would smell this way—like the dust that rims our shoes and spools in the corners of the park where our brooms never could reach.

They didn't invite us to the burial. Or maybe we just didn't feel right going. We never made our way up the narrow cement steps of the church into that open vestibule, air brighter there than it will ever be out here. Instead, we watched them carry the caskets, saw the long slick cars open their doors in the distance, while our hands kept to our pockets and our fingers touched gum wrappers and cigarette packs, folded and refolded dollar bills.

The skin on our hands is cracked and worn. The flags fly half-mast. We don't know their names. Don't know where they're from, although we imagine their homes are far away, inside skyscrapers or six- and seven-bedroom houses with stately lawns that grow grass year-round. They chose to come here. To eat our food and ride our rides.

We wait for someone to come and collect us. Tell us what to do. The church bells ring, and we see nothing from where we stand. We bow our heads. Clasp hands and say a silent prayer. Our hands feel one and the same.

SKIN

TEENSY'S INSIDE A BAD DREAM when the hammering on the door begins. He pulls on yesterday's pants and rubs his face. The clock on the dresser says it's 1:06 a.m., and no good comes of nighttime visitors. "Coming," he says to the pounding, turning lamps on as he moves through the hall. The dream lingers, and he notes the feel of his feet on the cool floor. Reminds himself that he's in his own house and the memories of the fire were from a long time ago. But then he unbolts the door and sees John Gardner standing beneath the porch light. The two haven't exchanged words in years. Teensy's confused. He's about to speak when he notices a pair of bare legs slung over Gardner's elbow, black ankle boots with heels like slabs of rock. It's Luann—his daughter—and his breathing thins. "Is she alive?" he asks, holding a hand above Luann's mouth. He feels warm air and tries to compose himself.

"She's passed out," Gardner says, stumbling in, smelling of booze.

Teensy's hands tremble as he goes to take Luann from Gardner, then stops. Even though Teensy is the one who cut the crusts off her sandwiches and sat up with her all night in a steamy shower when she had the croup, she's steady in Gardner's arms, and Teensy lets him go on holding her.

Luann has dyed her hair even darker—the blue-black of shoe polish—and it makes her skin eerie pale, like something left outside too long. To settle himself, Teensy touches the warpled skin below his shirt that runs from the base of his neck to just above his chest. It's an old habit, and he doesn't realize he's doing it until he notices Gardner glancing at him with cool distaste.

"Where should I put her?" Gardner asks. Teensy leads him to the bedroom, turns on a lamp. The air is still ripe with sleep. There are piles of dirty clothes and stacks of old magazines.

Teensy watches Gardner place Luann's head on the crumpled pillow. His jeans look pressed, and he's wearing a multicolored sweater. Teensy doesn't know when he last changed the sheets.

After Gardner leaves the room, Teensy yanks off Luann's boots. Her toes are red and crumpled, and he begins to work them through. The boots are cheap and don't fit well, and this realization saddens him more than her being passed out. He pats the covers around the outline of her body, and then he stands there, watches her breathe. All of Luann's years have settled around the bottom of her face, and her chin looks pitted, but Teensy still sees her as he always has: as his and Tess's little girl. His hand goes under the neck of his shirt. His fingers play on the rubbled skin.

When Luann was a child, they developed a game surrounding his skin. She would make an imaginary potion, spoon clinking inside a glass, and then she'd smooth it over the warpled flesh. There you go, she'd say, her tiny hands moving over him. Tess already gone by then and Luann's touch feeling delicious. You're all better now, she'd announce. Thank you, he'd say, smiling at her pleased face. It was only the two of them then, and he was so aware of Tess's absence, so wrapped up in his loneliness, its sudden agony. It felt like Luann's hands were really Tess's, saving him from this dark place.

Teensy hasn't seen Luann since the trial months ago, and she is thinner now than she was even then. He thinks about what the next morning might hold as he steps into the living room and sees John Gardner standing there. "You got anything to drink?" he asks.

Teensy blinks. "You bastard," he yells and lunges for Gardner.

With one swift motion Gardner jerks his elbow and knocks the wind out of Teensy, sends him flat on his back. He remains there, peering at the ceiling. He holds his throat, pets the skin. A weird tingling paws his chest as the air returns. "You're crazy, man," Gardner says. "I didn't do anything to her."

"Bullshit. I don't believe you."

"Truth. Jeez." Gardner smooths the front of his sweater, then puts a hand out to Teensy. Once he stands, Teensy releases air from his mouth, then shakes his head, takes a few steps to one side, then the other. "I found her at Katy's three sheets to the wind. Honest."

Teensy goes to the kitchen and takes down the bottle of whiskey from the cabinet over the stove. He fills two jelly glasses and brings them over to where Gardner has seated himself on the sofa. "Get the whole bottle," Gardner says. "I've got a story."

Teensy does as he is told and sets the bottle on the table before Gardner, when he realizes whom he is taking orders from. He straightens. "I appreciate what you did," he says. "Bringing her here. Now I think you should leave."

"I just got here."

"You're drunk."

"Not as drunk as her," and now Gardner chuckles, a sound gone gravely from tobacco. He tips his head back, and his peppered stubble gives him a prickly appearance.

"Okay, that's enough." Teensy grabs his arm and makes him stand. Gardner quiets with Teensy's hand on him. They are the same height, Teensy notices. All these years later, and he has finally caught up to Gardner.

"No reason we can't talk nice. We're grown men," Gardner reminds him. "Let's let bygones be bygones."

He drops Gardner's arm, gestures at the couch. Gardner smiles, lifts his drink. "To the old days," he says and empties his glass.

✳

After the fire that claimed everyone but him and his brother, Teensy—at age ten—went to live with the Gardner family. Twice a day Gardner's mother took his hand and led him to the second-floor bath, where she applied salves and clean bandages to the burned skin on his chest. Her eyes watered at the stench.

Gardner's mother, her voice as gentle as a summer breeze, told him he had a new life and that he could choose to remember as much or as little as he wanted. She talked sweetly to him. Murmured little things, petted the unharmed skin at the back of his neck, and the longer he stood there, the more bubbled up: the thick smell of it, smoke frying his eyes. Flames stripping everything in their house with clean heat. When she had no need to clean his oozing bandages, Teensy went to the bathroom alone and stood in front of the mirror. He watched the ugliness from the top of his chest to his right shoulder fill the mirror.

The bathroom became the only place where he was free of John Gardner's looks, his silent taunts. So, when the bathroom door whooshed open one day and Gardner busted the lock wide, Teensy should have expected it. "You stink," Gardner said, moving toward him. Teensy didn't say anything. He knew it was true. "You hear me? I said you smell like rot." Gardner pushed Teensy's shoulders. "I'm sick of you and your crappy smell." Teensy backed up until he hit the wall. "What you gonna do now?" Gardner's hands went for Teensy's neck. Teensy slid down, the air inside him going tight. Soon Gardner was on top of him, slap-fisting him. "I hate you! I hate you!"

Gardner's mother ran in then, tried to pull him off Teensy. "Quit it!" she yelled. Finally separating them, her hands already dabbing the goose egg at the back of Teensy's head. "After all he's been through," she said. "And now this? John Gardner, you should be ashamed of yourself." She turned Teensy's face to hers and bent down, her hand cupping his chin. Her voice muted. "Are you hurt?" She pulled him into her, held him tight, his breathing narrowed by her embrace.

*

The last time Teensy and Luann spoke, she'd called asking for money. It was hot then, just a few weeks after Footer's trial, when they locked him up for good, and when he'd refused, knowing she'd smoke it up, she called him an asshole, her spit smacking the receiver. Still, she's here in his house on this chill March evening. Frost whitens the windows. Teensy sees this as another chance to set things straight. He tries to sort his thoughts, but Gardner won't shut up.

"I was down at Katy's," he is saying, "having a drink at the bar. The juke was going, and Luann was dancing her heart out. Every song comes on, and she was dancing like it was just for her." Gardner takes a drink, empties his glass, and pours another. He gets a queer smile on his face that Teensy does not care for.

"So, Luann's having a great time. She doesn't seem aware of anything. Her hair's gone wet, and her eyes are kind of glassy. She has energy. I'll give you that. And in comes a group of ladies. Girls' night out. You'd know 'em—Chrissy Kenry and Joanna Rostarski and that whole crew. Remember them?"

Teensy cannot see faces, never one to recall names, but he senses them, remembers backing into a row of lockers as they pointed their fingers and laughed, how he hid beneath the bleachers, although it didn't make a difference. He kept the skin disguised beneath clothes, but this is exactly what they wanted to see. They always found him, dragged him to the bathroom, where they held him on the ground near the urinal, ripped off his borrowed clothes as he sprawled there, waiting for it to be over.

"They take a table and are drinking beer, and they start heckling Luann, calling her a baby killer. You shoulda seen her face. One minute she's dancing without a care in the world, the next thing they practically got her neck in a noose. She started crying. Not sure if it was the drink or what they said, but she was crying pretty hard."

"They hurt her?" Teensy asked, jaw tightening.

"Naw. Just said unkind things. I thought they were going to take Luann into the bathroom and rough her up. I had her come sit with me. She's a sweet girl," he said. "She calmed down for a bit until those pigs got a second wind, and they started chanting things, and we left." He perked his eyebrows. "Ever think about taking her somewhere else for a while?"

Teensy didn't like the sound of *we* coming from Gardner's mouth. Had the mind to say it was his daughter and Gardner didn't know the first thing about her. "I got friends all over," Gardner says. "Just gotta give it time, let this thing blow over."

Teensy hears a choked sound from the bedroom and runs. Arrives with both hands out, ready to resuscitate, the little he could remember from a mandatory training at Papermill. Luann has pushed her arms overhead, and pale blobs dab the edges of her mouth. She reclines on her back with abandon; her eyelids quiver, face both anxious and content. He didn't know she slept like that. If he woke her, those same eyes would settle on him, narrow, and her whole face would color with disgust. There is a chair in the corner. He wants to draw it bedside and keep her watch. She isn't drunk. There is more going on than that. Faint lines scale the inside of her arms. Most times when she asks for money, she tells him she is going to use it to go back to school. Says whatever she thinks he wants to hear.

He'd squandered lots of time worrying about bills, thinking about how he might have saved Tess. Maybe if he'd made Luann pancakes, talked more about her concerns, asked her questions about school—her teachers and friends—maybe he could have salvaged their relationship. But at the time it had all seemed inevitable: Bad things were always intended for him.

He touches the back of her hand and then returns to the tracked skin inside her arms. A lump rises in his throat that he can't swallow away.

*

Mr. and Mrs. Gardner told Teensy to forget Robert along with all the pain of remembering the time before now. But he knew his brother was out there—knew someone else was haunted by the same memories—and he did not take this fact casually. Teensy felt his faith filling him as he pushed heavy against the pedals of the donated bike, leaned into it with each turn. He knew by heart the way to the home of the couple that took in his brother. He was full of hope as he passed a spent farm. Thistles snagged his pant legs, but the house was there in the distance. Smaller than where he lived now with the Gardner family but neat and trim with painted shutters and a tree that flowered purple and scented the air.

It was a warm night, and the window to Robert's room was cracked. Teensy jimmied it further, enough to get his arms in and pull the rest of him inside. The house was quiet, the carpet plush. His brother had a stuffed dog tucked beside him. Robert looked smaller here, like he was growing in the opposite way. Teensy shook the boy awake. Gentle, then more insistent. He already envisioned holding his body on his back while steering the bike. He would need to be careful. Robert weighed next to nothing, and the road out to the rubble of what was their house wasn't paved.

When Robert opened his eyes, Teensy saw that they were gummed shut in places. He wet a finger to clear them, to help his brother see, but this was when Robert started screaming and even made Teensy frightened.

What's wrong? he asked while trying to shush him. Light spilled the room, and Mr. Cutler stood there in his underwear, holding his rifle. Mrs. Cutler spoke quiet. Made circles with her hand on Robert's back. His brother shivered in his bedclothes. His crying had given him the hiccups, and Mrs. Cutler rocked him on her lap.

Later Teensy overheard Mr. Cutler talking with Gardner's dad. Next time, he said, we'll call the police.

Next time, Mr. Gardner said, I'll call them myself.

*

Gardner has gotten comfortable with the whiskey. His tongue moves fast, slips out as he speaks. "My daughter Misty was a handful from the get-go. She was eleven or twelve—that ornery age—and I remember telling my wife she needed to do something, and my wife says, 'What makes you think I know what to do?'" Gardner snorts. "I took my sons outside. Taught them to ride and hunt and change the oil. Anytime something needed to be fixed, they were right there. But I didn't always get Misty."

Gardner stands, walks over to the cabinet where Teensy keeps his guns and a few books. He unlatches the door and takes out a rifle. He runs a finger down its stock, peers into the sight. "Haven't seen this in ages," Gardner says.

"It belonged to your dad."

"I know it." He watches Gardner handle the rifle, notes his clean unfettered skin, nails creamy white. Where he stands, legs parted, Teensy can see a shadow of the old Gardner. He sees his muscled legs. By sixth grade Gardner was taller and stronger than any other boy in their class. He's stout in the hips but belly barreled and just sixty. "He always did favor you," Gardner says, putting the gun back, closing the door. "They both did. My parents liked you best."

"That's not true."

"It's not?"

Teensy left Gardner's family just shy of graduation. Hitched a ride to Iowa City, then onto Illinois and Indiana, where he worked a series of odd jobs. Drove a school bus, worked beef cattle, picked peaches and apples at an orchard one year and painted houses and blew-in insulation the next. He was drawn to jobs that exposed him to sun and wind and rain.

"It tore my mom up. She used to sit in her chair doing her handiwork, but she was thinking of you. Wished you'd stayed."

Her face came to Teensy then. Settled before him in a kind of ghostly vision. After his burns healed, there was no need for Gardner's mom to tend to him, yet she continued to touch him—a hand on his arm, a few fingers grazing his cheek. She'd hold him in her eyes, make him look her square. He'd mostly stopped talking by then. Never was one for chitchat, but by high school he couldn't even stomach the sound of his own voice, how it hung dull and empty. Gardner's mother stroked Teensy's shoulder. She brushed her fingertips against the back of his hand years after the fire. You can talk to me, she said. Whatever you want to say, it's okay. Her touch became worrisome—full of something he could not name but felt in the back of his throat. Teensy fell further into himself, a silent abyss of hatred and disapproval that could only be solved by going away. Some of that disdain had remained, and Luann had picked up on it. She got on with that loser because she didn't have reason to believe there was anything better. He knew it for certain.

See, she was the way she was because of him.

*

After that ride to the home where Robert lived, they paid Gardner two quarters a week to be Teensy's chaperone, and he took him everywhere like some little pet. In fields that come summer would be tight with corn, Gardner instructed Teensy to smack the tall grasses with a stick. When he did so, rabbits spilled out the bottom. One, two, three. Gardner shot them with his gun, their bodies dropping heavy as loaves of bread. "Yes!" he hooted, gathering his prizes.

Teensy watched Gardner make a cut lengthwise down the center of the rabbit, then down its back. He peeled the skin so it hung from the ends of its paws, flesh pink as hamburger. As he skinned the last one, his hand slippery red, Gardner forced Teensy's fingers over the heart. It felt like a mouth trying to swallow him. "Come on," he said. "Let's go see the Polack."

Gardner placed the rabbits in a mesh bag and clipped it to his belt. They got back onto their bikes, and Teensy followed Gardner into town, where the streets were paved and the land was broken by rows of houses. They dropped bikes beside a white clapboard house and rattled the door. An old man in an undershirt and sweatpants waved them in with an unlit pipe.

Gardner dropped the rabbits on the kitchen table. The old man scooped the skinned bodies onto a metal bin and then took a wad of bills from his pants, counted some out, and handed them to Gardner. *Dobry!* Good, the man said, and gestured toward the couch. Gardner sat, and Teensy followed.

The man got out three juice glasses and filled each with a clear liquid. Teensy sniffed the drink, and the inside of his nose burned. "Come on, priss," egged Gardner. Teensy downed it, and by the end of his first glass, there was warmth in his belly that hadn't been there before.

Gardner raised his empty glass, yelled "Yee-haw!" at the TV, where a ballgame played. The old man grinned. Teensy noticed that he was missing a front tooth and the other one was gold. The light from the lamp struck it, and it winked at Teensy in a friendly way. *On jest pijany*, the man said, pointing at Gardner and laughing. His belly shook.

The old man lifted the bottle by the neck and refilled their glasses. Gardner grinned at Teensy, held his glass with two hands, and Teensy smiled back. He thought maybe Gardner didn't hate him after all. The sound from the TV sang in his ears. The afternoon sun shifted through the dingy windows, and everything seemed bubbly and carefree.

The door opened, and another man came in. Although he was younger, he resembled the old man in the gummed meat of his face and husked brows. He pointed at them. "Out!" he growled. "Get your asses out of here!" Gardner and Teensy scrambled to their feet. Gardner got to the door first, but the latch wouldn't release. "Gonna be sick," he murmured, fumbling with the door. He turned his face into his sleeve, and everything came out in hot pink chunks.

"That's disgusting," the younger man said. "You better clean it up." He shoved Gardner into the mess, then grabbed Teensy by the collar, exposing his chest. "What happened to you?" he asked. "You're an ugly fuck."

When Teensy and Gardner finally got home, it was dark, and dinner had already been put away. "Where were you two?" asked Gardner's dad.

"It was him," Gardner pointed. "I was chasing after him."

Gardner's dad's mouth slitted. "You. I'm getting tired of *you*." He grabbed Teensy by the ear, took him down the steps that led outside, and told him to unbuckle his pants and lean over. Teensy did as he was told. Air billowed beneath his undershorts.

The first slap of the belt, and he felt like he was being cut into pieces. He thought of the rabbits from earlier that day, the red meat of their flesh picking up crumbs on the old man's table. He turned his head to the side and saw a brilliant prick of stars in the night sky. Each thwack of the belt shook him. Teensy clung to his knees to keep from toppling.

Gardner's mother stood in the distance. "That's enough now," she pleaded. "He's just a boy."

Gardner's dad got into a rhythm, but even then Teensy could sense that he was working at something that had nothing to do with him. After what seemed like forever, Gardner's mother flung herself outright in front of the belt, taking a smack for him. "You and your little boyfriend, eh?" Gardner's father stopped then. He wiped at his forehead, threw the belt on the ground, and stomped off.

Gardner's mother helped Teensy up the stairs and into bed. She touched the skin at his neck, hummed some tune. He wanted to push her away. Gardner was in the bed beside him, and Teensy would pay for every perceived slight. Teensy leaned on his side, the only place that didn't ache. Leave me alone, he thought, unable to utter a word.

*

Something taps his feet. Gardner has rolled the empty bottle across the floor. "What else you got," he asks.

Teensy motions with his hands to show that's it. Gardner looks at him a second, maybe trying to determine if he's telling the truth.

"Guess I should call it a night." Gardner rises from the sofa, and the fabric bunches where he sat. He yanks at the waistband of his jeans, and the fat that clips over the edge slips back into his trousers. "Let me know how she is," he says. Teensy says sure, although he knows Gardner will not be coming out this way again. At the door Gardner turns, says, "Take care," and raises a hand.

Back inside the bedroom, Luann snores. She has turned her body toward the window. Teensy grabs a shirt from the ground and tents it over the lamp, mutes the light further, then pulls the quilt back up around her shoulders. It's a blue patchwork that he and Tess used when they were first married. A gift from someone, maybe Tess's mother.

He remembers when Luann's body first shifted, began to lengthen, hips growing wider—dear Lord, breasts. How frightening it had been to see her changing. It brought up Tess all over again. Life's great tragedies seemed rooted to the body, its unwieldy form.

With Luann's head twisted like that, it is easy to see the youth in her—that unmarred face. It is thin, yes, but the skin is whole and smooth like something that has slid from a pod. Teensy touches his neck as he watches her back rise and fall. The walls of his house are tired, the windows leak heat and wind whistles from them, but she is here.

TEENSY'S
DAUGHTER

GARDNER HEARS DOGS SCRAMBLING UP THE TREES after a squirrel or a neighbor's cat, he tells himself, eager to be calmed. It's not Teensy, he thinks. The same thing he's been telling himself for months. Teensy doesn't want anything to do with him. Isn't the sort who craves revenge.

Snow whisks fat heads of wildflowers gone brown with seed, while Gardner sits in his slippers, staring down a bottle of gin. Hard muscled and lean, he could pass for a man half his age except for the coarse white beard that he tugs as he thinks of his grown kids around a table heaped with casseroles, doing shots, laughing, chatting about remember whens. It's Christmas Eve. They wanted to spend it with their mother. The youngest one calls to tell him the news. Come meet us for drinks afterwards, Misty says, naming a bar—his bar—along the Black River. And while he'd like nothing more than to pull up a chair beside the three of them, beers and full shot glasses jiggling with golden light, it's a bad idea. Runs a finger behind the plastic band at his ankle. Have you forgotten already? Gardner wants to ask.

You don't have to be such a downer, Misty says later that afternoon, the only one who visits, huffing bags of groceries up the steps to his back door, never takes off her coat, says she's cold, just like her mother with her jutting cheekbones, legs and arms overgrown, still as thin as she was in junior high. He tries to feed her. Offers a can of corned beef hash heated in his toaster oven, fries an egg. Whatever he offers, she refuses.

I'm sorry, he had said when he addressed the courtroom during the trial—and Gardner meant it. Whether or not Teensy or the rest of them heard him was beyond his control.

Gardner made Misty toast with strawberry jam. He put it on a plate and extended it toward her—or that had been his intention—but now he's standing here at the counter next to the sink watching the blue plumes of exhaust snake from her car as she backs out his gravel drive. Blacked out again—little spots of forgetfulness. Doctor said they may grow longer or may fade away altogether. *Couldn't be certain*—those were the exact words the doctor used while opening and closing his suntanned hands, hands that had never lifted a pickax over his head in negative windchill, blisters at the mouth of each thumb. All those years of schooling, and this was how he chose to phrase the crumbling of Gardner's mind.

Might as well be six feet underground.

Thoughts and memories arrive as regular as the yellow finch in the feeder outside his porch and just as quickly catch and stumble, and Gardner falls into black pits, booby traps of his own making.

The snow piles up, covers the base of trees and dresses the branch arms, weeds. Gardner'd like to tell Misty that Teensy's daughter has forgiven him. Can feel the news on the end of his tongue each time he sees her, but he knows they'd put him away for good if they knew.

You see: She's been visiting him.

Luann slips in the front door, nightgown frozen gray planks, her body bony but soft. Never met someone who gave off such heat while her skin remained cool to the touch, even in the middle of August. Gardner makes Luann sit on the couch. Covers her legs and shoulders with blankets he's pulled from his own bed. She shivers. Tells him to stop fussing. *I ain't a baby.*

I know that, he says. But her feeble shape, the raw knobs of her knees, feet bare and ashen, he wants to do right by her. Teensy's daughter. For once Gardner wants to care for something, someone. He missed his kids' birthdays and school concerts. He was stuck in business meetings or involved in lengthy phone calls. He'd been full of himself then—health insurance, pension plan; his wife had seemed so much better with the kids. Her voice was tender. She was more interested in asking them questions and discovering their minds than he had been. Then, when his sons got older, after years of petty thefts, a group of men sitting at a long table decided that they needed to be taught a lesson. Both were sent off to the county school an hour away on Route 23. Never were the same after that. Wouldn't look him in the eye. His wife blamed him. Their marriage just a piece of paper then, already living downtown with one of her girlfriends.

But Teensy's daughter was different. Luann listened. He took her arms in his hands, traced the veins burrowed just beneath the surface. *Those drugs'll kill you,* he said.

You're always saying that.

It's true.

It's not. You did.

And his head gets all spotty, and the next thing he knows he is in bed with all his clothes on, window open at his bedside, tiny tornadoes of snow whirling on the sill, her smell on his fingers. Gardner rubs his head with the hand, wishes some of her might seep inside, heal him. Luann and Misty were in the same class in school, but he couldn't remember her from that time.

Daddy, she slept over on weekends! You drove us to the pool in the summertime. She gave me a ceramic unicorn for my twelfth birthday.

Still, he didn't remember Luann. But nearly a year ago he discovered her, parked in his cab in the unpaved lot outside Katy's Place. He'd retired by then and had started spending more time at the bar. Katy, who'd always been partial to him, let him keep a few personal items in a plastic bin behind the bottles. He supposed he'd seen Luann lurking near the door, grinding up against the juke even when it was silent. But she was as much a part of the bar as the stools and light fixtures, the Budweiser horse silently galloping on a shelf of varnished wood.

He was shocked by how nice his name sounded coming from her mouth. She crossed her legs, skirt too short, too tight, and asked where they were going.

Wherever you want to go, he'd said. And meant it.

I was hoping you'd say that, Luann said, as he fitted the key in the ignition, already feeling himself hardening inside his stiff jeans.

You pervert! Teensy had yelled, lurching toward him at the trial. The court-appointed attorney had separated them, unclenched Teensy's hands from the orange jumpsuit. It wasn't true. She'd been using for years, and everyone in town knew she kept a tent in the ravine beside the river, had been known to lift her skirt for twenty-five dollars. A few years ago news went around that boys from the college—fraternity boys—were driving down in a station wagon and parking along the ravine, building fires as tall as the lowest branches of the alders, drinking beer, a line outside the wind-whipped walls of her tent.

But the things they said didn't bother Gardner. He'd tried to save Luann. And Teensy must have known it. It had been sometime since they'd spoken. Teensy had a job working in the winder control room at Papermill after the company decided he was too old to drive the heavy miles, while Gardner tried his hand at investing.

Even before the fire, Teensy was the guy no one wanted to sit next to in class or on the bus. He used to find injured animals in the woods near his home and nurse them back to health in his daddy's barn. They pushed his books off his desk and spit wads of paper into his hair. Teensy never fought back, never flinched or teared up. Gardner, on the other hand, excelled at football, and everyone in his class wanted to tell him a joke, be his friend. It was Teensy's indifference that bothered Gardner most, like the rest of them didn't even matter.

Gardner recalled the day Teensy arrived on their doorstep, joined their family. It didn't make Gardner like him. He had that mismatched skin. They lived five years under the same roof, and except when his parents forced him to serve as his chaperone, they never interacted much at all until junior year of high school, when Teensy joined the swim team that Gardner captained. Gardner and the rest of his teammates had been doing laps at the Y since they were eight, racing in meets on weekends. Decorating their bedroom walls with ribbons. Then Teensy walked onto the pool deck in his too-long swim trunks, his messed-up skin right there for all to see. He dove into that cool abyss, barely able to keep his face in the water, yet there he was at every practice with his green towel. Gardner had long felt Teensy's gummy eyes and too-wide head following him in the halls of school; now they followed him on the deck and in the locker rooms, and it got to a point where Gardner had had enough.

Quit staring, freak! He once yelled between sets.

Gardner had friends. He went to parties on weekends. Girls liked him. And he was used to getting what he wanted.

Figured it'd be easy enough to scare him. So, Gardner told Teensy to join him at the pool over lunch. Said a group of them would be meeting before the conference meet. Hadn't planned what he was going to do, just knew he wanted to shake up Teensy.

That heavy stainless steel door shut behind Teensy, and he didn't even ask about the other guys. He just stood there on the pool deck in his cuffed jeans and overeager look as if he knew on some level what Gardner wanted to do to him.

What's up, chief? Gardner asked with a gentle wave of his hand, then struck quickly: He grabbed Teensy and flipped him over onto his back, stuck his piggish face beneath the water in the deep end. Gardner was so much larger, stronger, and with his hands fastened around Teensy's neck, fingers digging into the spongy mottled flesh, he realized he wanted more than to make Teensy nervous and force him to quit the team. He wanted to hurt him.

Somehow Teensy slid a leg up, kicked Gardner into the pool, the two of them wrestling underwater. And then Teensy stretched his arms out and pushed off, broke free of Gardner's grasp, and started swimming this crazy beautiful stroke. Gardner wasn't going to let him get off so easy. He reached toward him, Teensy's heels just beyond his grasp.

At the other end of the pool, Teensy pulled himself out in one fluid motion. Gardner's chest heaved. What the heck, man. Who are you? he asked from the water, still trying to catch his breath. Where'd you learn to swim like that?

But Teensy just stared at him, maybe the last time his eyes would rest on Gardner's. And then he walked out in his wet clothes, slipping down the halls of the school; didn't stop walking until he left town altogether. Gardner's parents said it was for the best when he upped and left. He was gone for a few years. Gardner heard he'd earned his GED. Found a girl, married her, and ended up back in Ingleside, where his wife's family had a farm. Tried to start a family. Teensy's wife got pregnant again and again but couldn't hold onto any of them. They adopted Luann, and then when she was four years old, Teensy's wife got pregnant, and every limb on her swelled like a balloon. She lost the baby at the hospital and didn't survive the week. The coffin was cream satin, and inside it Teensy's wife held the swaddled baby across her chest, his tiny hands clenched fists.

So, it was Teensy and his daughter in the old house until he lost the land and took the job with Papermill. Then he was on the road, and Luann would be alone with his wife's elderly mother. It wasn't until high school that Luann started disappearing, spending evenings at Glory Days and later showing her face on the dance floor at Katy's Place.

*

There are things Gardner wants to tell Misty. He's started a list. Keeps it in the pocket of his shirt. Sometimes he will misplace it, and a few days will go by, and during that time things come to mind, but when he finds the paper, he's forgotten what he wanted to say.

Misty has a boyfriend he's never met. He wants to shake his hand, look him face to face. Don't let him boss you around—that's the first thing on the paper. If he ain't nice, you walk away. Simple as that. But honestly, it isn't that easy to move on. His own wife should have kicked him to the curb years before she actually did. But you get used to each other, and even the bad stuff becomes familiar. Tolerable.

You remind me of someone, Luann said that first time they drove around the back roads in his truck. Drove the whole night all the way to Streatmore until the sky behind the hills turned purple so fast it was like someone switched on a light.

He hoped Luann didn't say her dad. Didn't think he could stomach the sound of Teensy's name while his hand rested on her bare thigh.

My brother.

He didn't kiss her that first night even though he wanted to. By the time the sun reflected on the hood of the car, his eyes were growing heavy. He dropped her off outside Katy's Place. Fixed himself a ham sandwich at home and stumbled into bed. He woke hours later with a start, something pinning him down. It was her straddling him, one hand pressing his chest.

I lied about my brother. You don't remind me of anyone. And then she kissed him on the mouth, taste of her like chewed-up sale papers, her warmth against his skin. Couldn't recall the last time he'd been with a woman, white hairs springing from his chin. He was an old man. Figured she was lonely, would take up with someone else as soon as the wind changed directions. He would enjoy her as long as she let him. That was the initial plan.

But watching Luann stumble in without a coat or shoes, he started to buy her things. She'd sit on his lap on the couch, and he'd slip one of his socks over her foot, slide that foot inside a new gym shoe. She'd stay with him for days—would get sober— but then Gardner would wake, and he'd find the red sweatshirt he'd pulled over her head slung over the arm of the couch, and she'd be gone. When she wasn't there, he felt off-center. He'd see her at Katy's Place on a binge, eyes half-open, makeup smeared, sweet-talking any guy who came up to her. He wanted her to look at him, just a few feet away, sucking down one whiskey after the other, wanted some sort of recognition for their time together.

And it was during these gaps that he started to drink more. Began stocking up at the liquor store, rows of bottles beneath the kitchen sink clinking together to make room for the next. He started thinking about things that happened long ago— remembered his father taking off his belt, whacking his backside, his mother's cool hand against his fevered forehead. Had he ever told his kids about the pork chops his grandmother used to make, vermouth simmering on the bottom of the pan, meat falling off the bone? He was at a wedding at the VFW the first time he met their mother. She was wearing a yellow dress with a bow beneath her small breasts, and he'd asked her to dance, and when he placed his hands around her waist, he'd felt a jolt not unlike an electric shock.

But then Gardner would see one of his sons pumping gas or filling some guy's tires, and they'd exchange a wave, a few pleasantries, and the words that were meant to follow eluded him.

It was easier to talk to his daughter. He'd call her up and invite her to meet him for coffee. Once or twice Misty did just that, and during the first twenty minutes or so, he'd note the hard edge around her mouth. Knew he was responsible for that anger.

There are so many mistruths passed for fact. He wishes Misty could step inside his mind and see what he has seen: the one time he walked in on Luann slumped over on his toilet, needle still nosing its way in her forearm. He grabbed her chin, shook her awake, and the first thing she did was spit a goober smack in the middle of his face. She told him he was a piece of shit and started hitting him all over. His lip cut open, blood dribbling his shirt. Her hands were so cold. He put his army jacket over her shoulders, figured if he could warm her, get her to eat something, she'd be okay. But her eyes kept flipping back. Gardner called an ambulance, and then out of fear that strikes only fools, he called Teensy. He cradled Luann on his lap, propped her head up on his shoulder. He was holding her that way when Teensy waltzed in. What she on? he asked, hands hidden deep in his coat pockets.

He didn't know. Told Teensy to check the bathroom, said that's where he'd found her.

Teensy shrugged. Little up-and-down motion with his shoulders. His daughter drooped across the body of another man, and the guy—Teensy—just stood there.

Ain't my problem anymore, Teensy said. Shook his hands. I'm done. Said it quietly at first, like he was trying out how it might sound. Done! Hear me? He bent toward her, eyes ringed black, breath sparse and shallow, just a strawful of air slipping between her lips. Anything you touch is tainted, he said, and he spat on the ground and walked out.

To this day Gardner wasn't clear to which of them Teensy spoke.

The back door heaved shut before the van pulled up, red lights flashing. They laid her flat on the rug like a doll, something disposable, snipped off her shirt in two seconds; a man in the navy cap that skimmed his skull slapped her arm, every vein shot. Put hot packs on Luann's feet and finally found a way inside her.

What's your daughter on? they asked.

Gardner winced. He should have told them right then it wasn't like that.

You see, he loved her.

*

The black spaces are irregular. A few days will go by, and Gardner's mind will work just fine. He'll put seed in the feeder, mend his pants. Heat a can of soup for lunch. Read some of the previous days' newspaper. Think about things. Add a few notes to the list. And he'll think: Maybe the doctor was wrong. Maybe I'm just tired. I've healed myself, he thinks. Feels his mood improve. Thinks about changing into his camouflage and going hunting, fixing his rifle in the holder inside the truck's cab, stepping into the hushed openness of the woods. Went so far as to pack a cooler, dug his sleeping bag out of the shed in back when the transmitter began to buzz, followed by a phone call from his sponsor. They were speaking on the phone, and he was telling him a story—he didn't know about what—and the next thing he knew, he woke in a cold shower fully dressed two days before Christmas.

Luann? Luann? He called, stringing a towel around his waist, teeth chattering, moving from room to room looking for her.

She's dead, Daddy, Misty said when she came in that afternoon to find him dressed in still-wet clothes. She's not coming back.

She didn't even flinch to see Gardner in his stringy damp undershorts. She helped him into dry clothes, patted his arm real gentle. Made him a cup of instant coffee. Heated the cream.

Daddy, she said. Do you remember what happened to Luann? He looked away.

This is important, she said. Think real hard. What do you remember?

It was the one thing he had been unable to forget.

*

After her hospitalization Luann was better. Swore she was done using. Threw out the pencil case she used to hold her drug paraphernalia. She took long baths, and he leaned over the side of the tub and lathered her hair, rubbed the spaces between her toes. Sometimes she opened her legs and he got right in the tub with her, pressed his back up against her bare chest, the two of them wet and slippery, her hands fastened around his chest.

Summer rushed in. They opened windows and planted a garden out back. Ate salads for dinner. She made a pie with wild berries. Her first. They drove to Welmann's together and bought groceries. Took walks, held hands. Her face filled in, hair grew out in long, soft waves. Every day she looked younger. Meanwhile, dark caverns blossomed under Gardner's eyes, skin at his neck bunched like a sweater. He seemed to be aging overnight. Waking with her feet against his was a little bit of Eden, but he couldn't stop worrying about her. He wanted Luann to be happy. He wanted to give her what he'd been unable to provide anyone else.

One morning she said she wanted French toast, but they were out of bread. She said she couldn't go on with the day without it, and so she took the keys to his truck, headed down to Welmann's. Thinking back, she was gone longer than necessary. And when she returned, she was shaking. He held her real tight, thought maybe she was coming down with something. When she complained of a headache, he told her to take a nap, and he spent the rest of the morning in the shed out back, where he was making her a birdfeeder, something to tend to.

When she woke, her eyes darted everywhere but to his. She headed out the door not long after. Must have pawned the ring he'd given her. Wasn't even certain she was wearing it that morning.

After everything it comes down to that band of gold, the sapphire stone set between two diamonds. It should have gone to Misty. It had belonged to his mother and his mother's mother before that. Maybe his mind had betrayed him that day as well. The moment he'd flipped off the TV and hopped down on one knee, asked for Luann's hand. She'd nodded and started crying, took him into her outstretched arms.

But he can't trust his mind any longer. Isn't certain what comes out of it is tied to reality in any way. He could ask Misty and hear one thing. He could call Teensy and apologize for everything, like his counselor and the people from AA have encouraged. His grandmother used to tell him if you do good, you get good. So, how long, he wonders, will he be paying for his mistakes?

*

Fall came, and with it Luann returned for shorter and shorter intervals. From then on she was always strung out. She didn't want him to touch her, and she didn't want to eat. She'd sleep for a day and a half straight and when she woke craved cheap packaged cookies. Cigarettes. He'd never liked to smoke, couldn't stand the smell of it on his clothes after being at Katy's Place, but he let her light up while stretched out on his couch, feet propped up on pillows, anything to keep her happy. So thin at that point her shoulders would slip out the neck of her T-shirt.

You think I am the only one for you, but there are hundreds of girls just like me, she said.

That's not true.

It is. Drive the city streets. See them lurking against cold brick, breath a fine-veiled thing. They can make you feel good.

That's not what I like about you. And he motioned toward the bedroom, bed still warm from where he'd lifted himself off of her twenty minutes prior. But he never knew what she saw in him.

Everyone wants to feel invincible. We aren't that different.

He didn't like what she'd said. Made him question how many others there had been. One time he'd asked her about the drugs, why she used.

Why not? You the police? And she'd stepped into another room, shut the door, and blocked him out.

*

Fact is the black spots started soon after he'd emptied a drawer for Luann, put his socks and undershirts in the same cramped space. They usually began with a headache. His own mother had been eating a peanut butter sandwich for lunch, glass of iced tea in front of her, when the bubble entered her bloodstream, and one trellised branch of her brain suddenly flashed black.

Like mother, like son.

Gardner's made his share of mistakes. But he wants to tell Misty that he's tried to make amends. And that act of contrition, he believes, is as important as anything else.

He can't recall the last thing he said to Luann. So much of that night feels jagged and uneven. He had spent most of the day at Katy's Place. Had been passing the length of hours there, sitting in his place toward the middle end of the bar, pushing a paper napkin back and forth, just being his usual sullen self, wondering where she'd gone this time, if she had collapsed in some dark alley and was calling for him. Once she'd told him he had saved her, and he couldn't get those words out of his thick skull, the weight they carried once they hatched in his ears.

He sat there thinking of all the places she might be and was going to sit there a little more and then go look for her. He'd finish his whiskey—maybe have one more, he was thinking, when the door swung open, a tinkle of bells, her giggling. There was a meaty co-ed with a crew cut in front of her, two behind. This didn't stop Gardner from jumping up, grabbing hold of her elbow, trying to steer her back to him. Something horrible clenched up inside him when he saw Luann there.

He's no expert on the ways of women, Gardner wants to tell Misty, but you can't profess your love to someone and then take it away and not expect there to be some consequence. Maybe more than anything else, Gardner wants her to really hear him on this one: Don't toy with someone's emotions. Not like what Luann did that night at Katy's.

Maybe they were all strung out. Who knew how long the group had been together, what they'd been doing. The first two guys barely looked at him, didn't seem bothered by his putting an arm around Luann's back, guiding her to his warm stool. Her hand so cold inside his. It was the end of October then, and she was wearing flip-flops, just like the ones she'd worn all summer while rocking on his porch.

Let's go home, Luann. This is no place for you to be, he said.

She wrung her hands out of his grasp and stood up straight. He hadn't noticed it before, but she was just as tall as him when she pushed her shoulders back.

I don't owe you shit, Brylcreem.

He let her walk away, back to the booth where her friends had covered the table in pitchers of beer and bags of salted nuts. He stood there for some minutes, stunned. Got angry. Thought about hoisting her over his shoulder and carrying her right out of Katy's Place. But Gardner's own feebleness stepped in, and he returned to his seat. Ordered a round of drinks for the table; he knew she'd like that. Gardner nursed his own drink while his eyes were on them.

At the trial they put Katy on the witness stand. Called up all three of the college kids in their fancy suits, with their city lawyers. Again and again they asked if Gardner seemed angry with Luann, if they'd exchanged harsh words. The smallest of the three seemed most thoughtful. But they were all liars. They said that when Luann came back to the table, Gardner's handprint was on the top of her arm. One of them said he could remember the white etch slowly filling in, and when they offered to teach Gardner a lesson, Luann had just laughed at the idea. When they'd asked Luann who he was, the old dude near the end of the bar, beard white as Santa, she said she never saw him before in her life, but she'd tipped her glass to him when Katy brought over the fresh round of drinks.

Just another stranger buying her a beer.

Gardner could hold his liquor better than any of them. So, he waited them out. Devised a plan. Or plans. Knew if he could get her home and pile every blanket he owned on top of her, warm her up, she would come back to him.

Now when they talk about that night, Luann says it was when she understood love.

Because you wanted me to fight for you, he says.

No baby, just the opposite. I didn't want any harm to come your way. But it still did.

Well, that was your own doing. That was the risk you took on, she says, leaning into him, curling her lips around the flap of his earlobe. *Wasn't this worth it?* she asks, in the fold of his lap.

*

Last call, 2 a.m. Katy turning on the high lights, shooing everyone out the door with a dish towel. There were only two guys left with Luann at that point. Gardner knew if she got into a car with them, he'd never see her again.

He followed them out. Watched Luann get in the backseat with the blond one, waited until he was pulling the door shut, then leaned right over him, lifted her out. The guy was too drunk to even know what was going on.

Like a baby, he said.

Like a princess, she corrected.

And she immediately warmed to Gardner, kissed his face all over, let him buckle her into his cab, tuck a blanket over her legs. Her fruity breath. They started the ride home.

It had rained earlier in the week; mud had frozen in places, lumps of ice, fallen branches, every tire rotation like going up a curb. What did they talk about as they drove, everyone in the courtroom wanted to know. It seemed so frivolous now, he had to admit, but then it had felt like three steps forward, like in his presence she was instantly sober. She was telling him how she used to do the hair of all the girls in the high school bathroom before classes began, had a case she carried with her, filled it with sprays and mousses and brushes. She said she thought she could do hair for a living. Knew of a program she could attend part-time, said the tuition wasn't cheap.

How much is it, he asked, already willing to write her the check there and then. He wanted to keep the conversation going.

But he *was* angry with her on some level. Wanted to make her ask for what she wanted. It wasn't the first time he'd given her money, but it would be the first time she asked. He was driving fast, he'd admit that. Trees breezed past, a few crumpled hands of leaves skirting along the windshield, the Black River bubbling below, a murky ominous thing. He was asking her what she'd do if she earned her certificate.

I'd open my own shop, and she reached over, lifted a few pieces of his hair, and rubbed them between her fingers. You know, I could do something for you, she was saying. Get this hair to behave real nice.

And then a spot erupted in his mind, a monumental burst, and everything went forever dark.

*

He wants to sit the three of his kids down right here at his kitchen table and tell them how he clawed around for her, truck upside down and sinking slowly, how he stuck his face in the frigid water, eyes blinking past the black murk of car oil and litter, looking for her, chill so great, limbs nearly immovable. *Luann!* he screamed. *Luann! Where are you?*

They said she'd been thrown out of the truck. Misty cut out the articles that stated so, fixed them on the refrigerator with magnets. He wasn't sure if she did this to help him or hurt him.

FATAL INJURIES TO LOCAL WOMAN

ALCOHOL SUSPECTED IN DEATH OF MOTHER

That second one puzzled him most. He asked Luann about it the last time she spent the night. *So what*, she said. *You think you were the only one?*

I didn't know you had a kid.

Big deal. Doesn't everyone?

No matter how many times he has apologized, Gardner wonders if she really has forgiven him like she says. She seems angry, and he wishes he could help her understand that night, how after the police placed him in a cell, she was all he could think about. Later they released him to his house, head bandaged like a sick dog, and he walked from room to room, opened every drawer and cabinet, searched for a sign Luann had once been there. He was certain on some level she was hiding, standing alone in the woods waiting for the perfect moment to jump out and return to him. He waited. Days passed. When she didn't appear, he lined up on the counter every bottle of prescription pills he'd ever received and stood there with a glass of water. Luann had made clear what his life had been missing. There was no point continuing. But with each fleeting minute he became more certain that he couldn't let Misty find him sprawled on the linoleum, pants filled with his own crap.

So he stopped eating. He dropped twenty pounds in a matter of weeks, had to use a rubber band to keep up his pants. The sight of food—a slice of lunch meat or even a hunk of bread— made him vomit. Misty brought over cases of protein shakes and would hold the uncapped bottle under his mouth until he took a drink. But with his thin frame, you couldn't deny it: He began to resemble Luann.

All of this has not been in vain, Gardner tells Misty. He's not drinking anymore, and now when Luann isn't around, he mostly sits at the table with a deck of cards or that sheet of notebook paper and pen figuring out what else he has to say. If it hadn't been for Luann, his own daughter wouldn't be visiting him now, would she?

And while he'd like nothing more than for Luann to stay with him, it's no longer safe. Misty lifts her eyebrows when she walks in and he and Luann are talking. The counselor asks about Gardner's state of mind. He's talked to the doctor, knows about the blackouts. Part of his reduced sentence is dependent upon the doctor's statement that the mass in his brain continues to expand.

But Gardner sees it differently. He imagines the part of his brain consumed with Luann taking up more and more space. Sees it as a giant puddle refusing to dry up, go away. Every time the black spots appear, swallowing him, he knows it's Luann trying to get back to him. He just hasn't figured out how to get her to stay.

DOWNER

EVERY POUND TEENSY HAD GAINED in the past few months jiggled on the uneven road. Crumpled wax paper from that morning's two breakfast sandwiches rolled beneath the gas pedals, an empty box of donuts on the seat beside him; still, hollowness remained. He drove on Route 26 and followed the river. Teensy wondered if his daughter would like an overlook or if Luann would prefer to rest right in the water, her ashes lapping the shore. His cravings increased with each bend in the road. Even now Teensy didn't know where to leave her.

He wanted a strawberry shake and some French fries in a paper cup. Longed for rolls that sprung from a can, baked in little triangles and slathered with butter right from the oven. Hadn't he always told Luann breakfast was the most important meal of the day? Now he would sit down to mealtime—a drive-thru bacon cheeseburger or one of those ready-made dinners that came in a box—and he'd start shoveling in the food, and for those few moments the ache of remembering would be blunted. While Teensy ate, he would think of things he had long neglected. The leaves needed to be emptied from the gutters and the front door latch—it hadn't worked right in years, and today he was going to fix it! These thoughts would brighten him. He could pass another day. But then he scraped the bottom of the tinfoil plate, tines of his fork bringing up nothing but grease, and he knew he wouldn't do a thing. Some men his age liked nudie magazines. Others, like Gardner, hit the bottle. Teensy's weakness was inside a Hungry-Man dinner.

The road dipped, and Teensy shifted to a lower gear and then gave it gas. The heifers they'd purchased from a guy in Des Moines would arrive midday. He had promised Gardner he'd be there well in advance, but by the shifting daylight he knew he would be late. He came to a split where the trees had been cleared and took a turn. Newer developments stood empty, as extinct as the corn and soybeans that once sprouted the land, while the roads leading to them were black and smooth. When they traveled this path, the urn remained steady and upright, belted beside him in the truck. Fortunately, most of the roadway remained rough and pitted, and he was obliged to keep a hand on the bronzed pot to keep it from toppling.

The sun rose higher, melting icy veils that still rimmed the shore of the water below. Teensy made a neat circle, taking Route 64 up to Pruewood, turning around, and following the river back. He knew Gardner would be checking his watch and maybe even cursing Teensy. Just thinking about it pissed him off. If it hadn't been for Teensy forgiving him and Gardner's tumor, Gardner would still be behind bars.

He was well beyond the speed limit, gravel pinging into the bed, when the truck hit some gouge. Teensy's head smacked the window. He rubbed the bones of his face, could feel a bruise blossom. He did the loop three or four times, until he had to roll up the windows and blast the heat high just to get his reddened fingers to bend. Teensy's stomach grumbled. He couldn't do it much longer. Thoughts exploded in his mind—all of it happening again—the phone call from the police, the drive out to the coroner, the sound of the heavy zipper, and then the sight of Luann's limp arm resting across her gray-blue skin. He pulled over, grabbed the urn, and got out between two signs, one with NO TRESPASSING and the other DUCK CROSSING.

He hiked out to a steep overlook, river right below him. Teensy didn't know if this was Ingleside or some unincorporated part of town. He held the urn to his chest, took a deep breath, and yanked off the top. In his mind Teensy saw himself tip the pot, holding it by its heel as the ashes unfurled in a dark pearly swath—only he couldn't do it.

He refitted the lid. He was too weak even now. Teensy held the metal urn tightly to his chest and swiped at his nose. If Gardner weren't expecting him, if the heifers weren't slated to arrive that day, he'd speed as fast as he could to the nearest drive-thru and bury his sorrow in the pillowy softness of a sesame seed bun.

*

"What happened to you?" Gardner huffed when he finally answered the door to his house. Teensy watched Gardner paw at his eyes, and he knew he just woke. Teensy imagined the tumor as a brick squashing his brain and all the life out of him. Gardner wheeled himself to the side to let Teensy pass but then rose out of the chair and took a crumpled stance behind a walker. The skin on his arms flapped loose as he pushed the skeleton-like contraption. Teensy still hadn't gotten used to seeing Gardner this way.

They had shaved his head with the last surgery, and the hair had failed to grow back. His scalp shined, the scar a bright pink. Gardner had tried to grow a beard, perhaps to offset his denuded state, but the white stubble was patchy. Beneath it Teensy could see the edges of his face. Gardner was full of edges now. He couldn't cinch the belt of his pants any tighter, and so he had twisted the end of the leather until it hung in front of him like a tail. The Gardner of yesteryear would have waltzed in and pushed his current self over. But they were both old men now, and the past, Teensy reminded himself, was nothing more than the past.

Teensy stood on the rug just off the door and stuffed his hands inside his jacket pockets. He had left the urn fastened inside the truck's front seat. Despite all of Gardner's goodwill and his apologies, Teensy couldn't bring Luann back inside here.

It was time to move on. They had gotten a good deal on fifty heifers purchased with Gardner's money, and they were getting a bull from a guy in Savoy later that week. Teensy would be responsible for cultivating the herd on Gardner's land, like previous generations. Gardner didn't have much time left, and this was his attempt to right some of his wrongs. "They should have been here by now," Gardner spurted. "You sure this is the day?"

Teensy set his jaw. "Positive."

Gardner repositioned his weight on the walker. "Well, there's soup," he said, lifting his chin to motion toward the kitchen. "It's good too. The girl was out. Something with bacon and beans. You'll like it." And as he said the last part, he clamped his hands like a vice around his skinned head and scrunched his eyes shut. He wavered. The couch was right there, and he somehow slumped into it.

"You okay?" Teensy asked. "Want some water or something?" He stood there and waited. Gardner did not respond but stretched out, eyes shut tight. The longer Teensy stood there watching him, the dumber he felt, hands hanging at his sides. Teensy told Gardner that he was going to go outside and check on things. As he closed the door behind him, he heard Gardner murmur, "Should have been here by now."

Teensy hustled down the steps, anything to get away from the man and fast. He had convinced himself he could do this— work with Gardner for the little while he had left. Teensy tried to muster some pity and fix in his mind the picture of Gardner's whittled body. But every time Teensy felt a sliver of sympathy for Gardner, the man ignited in sudden anger. "I won't take offense if you aren't interested," Gardner had said that day months ago when he'd gone over to Teensy's rented house with his lawyer, and the guy stood there in a suit and tie on his doorstep, and Teensy, who had been two frozen meals into his dinner when he heard the knock on the door, had wondered who had died now. "I'm leaving it all to you," Gardner said, wobbling on the little rubber mat. He leaned on a cane with an ivory carving, but even that hadn't steadied him. It was a year after Luann's death, and Gardner had just completed his house arrest, but the second brain surgery had not been a success.

The next few minutes had been just like in the movies. The attorney unfolded the papers right there, and Teensy saw his full name—Timothy Michael Teensy—in black ink under the script at the top that read Last Will and Testament of John E. Gardner. "Ain't gonna be around forever," Gardner said. "I'll feel better knowing one thing will go on the way it should. You get the house, the land. You can raise cattle again. It's good pasture. You know it is. Some of the best in town."

Teensy didn't know what to say. Looked from the stranger to Gardner, who felt like one. "Don't have to decide now," Gardner said, his breath smelling of barbecue.

Part of him wanted to hear Gardner say it out loud: I killed your daughter, so I'm going to give you my land. But he didn't say that. "I don't understand," Teensy finally said, shifting weight from one foot to the other and handing back the papers.

"You don't have to," Gardner responded.

*

On the hillside, with the barn at his back, Teensy could see the frame of the Tornado. It was spring, and the newspaper editorials were talking again about reopening the park. He thought of all that fertile soil buried beneath cement and steel. Years ago, just as they began construction on Glory Days, he had heard that the developers paid the Gardner family a million dollars for the land. Now he knew that was only a fourth of the amount heaped in Gardner's bank account.

Teensy didn't think of himself as rich. It was Gardner's money, and Teensy was a farmer who raised beef cattle, only he had gone years without cows of his own. Teensy stood with the four horses inside the pen that extended from the side of the barn. It angled down an incline, stopping just before the trees thickened. He touched a horse behind her ears, watched her nostrils expand and contract. He refilled the trough with water, found the bag of oats on the inside wall of the barn near the flashlight and fed them this as well. In the corner stood Gardner's father's tractor, which he'd used last week to spread fertilizer on part of the pasture. He had never paid for commercial fertilizer, never had the means or the need to do so, but money was no longer a limiting factor.

Teensy was nearing seventy years old, and now it would be up to him to dig up the horse root and keep the heifers from the pigweed in the spring. Summer he'd plow for hay or pay someone else to. He'd put up wind fences late November and maybe see if he could hire someone to help out.

Farther out he heard the truck grind its gears, saw its headlights on the county road as it made its way toward the house. A giddiness rose up in him. Teensy took off his cap, repositioned it on his head, and started up the hill. He shook hands with the driver, and when the man said he'd gotten caught up in traffic on the interstate, Teensy nodded. "You're here now," he said and pointed where he wanted the driver to let down the ramp.

Teensy followed the driver to the back of the truck. He undid the latch, and the back gate swung up with a rattle and a chorus of moos. Teensy grinned. The first two heifers made their way down the metal ramp, hooves clicking like high heels, their bellowing amplified by nerves. "It's okay, ladies," Teensy said, letting his hand skim the bony protrusions of a heifer's back. Must be the runt, he thought, and he moved toward the new corral they'd had built, the wood as fine and clean as a baby's arm.

The pasture extended well beyond the barn, but for now the heifers clumped together, got the feel of solid ground. The floodlights came on, and their snorts and grunts filled his ears. With the last few heifers unloaded, the driver slid the ramp along the underside of the semi. He closed the doors and wished Teensy good luck.

"Don't need it!" Teensy chirped and then waved him off. The semi rumbled as it made its way down the gravel drive in the setting sun.

Teensy stood steady between the heifers. The ground was soft and flat and unrutted. He watched their jaws work as they ate the clover and sweetgrass that had just begun to come in. Their bellowing lessened; the light reflected off their inky coats. He could feel them splitting the air as they sidestepped him, their sounds as familiar as ever. He recalled how Luann would help him with the cows in the morning before school. The two of them would vaccinate the cattle in spring and supplement their feed in winter. They worked without talking. She was around ten or eleven years old then, and the bones in her face had begun to lengthen. She began to eat so much food, he had to go for groceries two, sometimes three, times a week.

He tried to refocus, return his thoughts to the work at hand. This time he wouldn't have to limit the heifers' time in pasture— Gardner's land stretched for miles in every direction. Tomorrow morning they'd work the squeeze chute, tag and weigh the heifers, give them their shots. Arbuckle's son was going to come out and help. His stomach gurgled unhappily, and Teensy thought about heading home. "I'll see you girls soon," he said, petting their backs, starting to walk toward the house, where he'd parked. He rubbed his neck as he walked. It ached from the morning spent hunched over the steering wheel. It would be good to get home.

"Getting settled," said the voice, and only then did Teensy see Gardner leaning on the walker several feet from the back door, binoculars dangling from his neck.

"Yup. I'll see you tomorrow," Teensy said. "Bright and early. You need a hand?" He was already thinking about heating up a Hungry-Man and how nice his bed would feel afterward.

"They aren't right," Gardner said, and Teensy, imagining himself in his own kitchen, pouring a glass of juice and cutting into a slice of steaming Salisbury steak, said, "What?"

Gardner was pointing with that shaking hand of his. "They are too puny for two years. Won't make a good herd."

Teensy stopped to look where Gardner instructed in the hours-gone sun. It's true that the heifers looked thin, scrawnier than he'd have liked, but he knew he could get them to where they needed to be. "Nothing some good pasture won't fix."

"Look closer," Gardner said, using his old man chin to direct. "Look at that one. Her legs are not right." As they stood there, one of the heifers sat in the middle of the others and mooed. Teensy squinted at her. "I've got to get the vet out anyways. Give everyone a once-over."

Gardner shook his head. "No way. Not for what we paid. They can come get the whole lot."

Teensy didn't know what to say. It had been years since he had herded up cows from the back of a horse or pregnancy-checked a heifer—but he could sense that part of himself deep below the surface. Knew that just like these heifers needed tending to that he, too, could be made over, extracted from his blubbery self.

"I'll get them on vitamins," Teensy said to Gardner. "And I'll call the vet tonight. We'll get them their shots, and the vet'll prescribe them some antibiotics. Then the alfalfa will come in and more clover, and all will be right and good."

He moved his flashlight along the herd, and it was true. They were a skinny, scrawny bunch, but that's why they got a bargain. He could fatten them up. He knew he could. All along he had been planning on heading home, bringing Luann's urn inside and letting the metal come to room temperature. Placing it on the table as he ate his boxed meal and then setting it on the bedroom dresser and getting some rest. Now Teensy knew he'd never leave. The sky would go black, the temperature would plummet, winter not too much in the past, but he couldn't leave them, not with how he was needed.

Gardner grabbed the flashlight out of his hand. "You see that?" A heifer rested in the dirt as the others stepped around her. She mooed but seemed unable to rise. Teensy moved to the heifer, tucked his feet under her, and kicked her with his knees. She remained down, and he grabbed the root of her tail with both hands and heaved upward. "Come on, sissy. Work with me," Teensy said, but the heifer didn't budge.

"She's a downer," Gardner announced.

"No she's not. Probably just got shipping fever. The drive was long. Some green grass and rest will fix her right up. She'll be fine."

"Rest is not gonna heal that. If it's pneumonia, she's gonna infect the whole herd, and then all this'll be a waste." Gardner waved at the surroundings with the front handles of his walker and nearly fell over. He snorted, a raw sound that startled the heifer nearest them and sent her trotting. "I get it now." Gardner slapped his thigh. "You almost got me, old man. Yes, sirree." He turned toward the house and started swinging his left arm like a baton, leaning on the walker and picking it right back up, moving faster than Teensy had seen him do in months. Teensy felt some of the old anger. He wanted to say that these were his heifers now and this was his land. Hadn't the will stated just that? Gardner had said that he hadn't much time left, that the tumor was growing bigger. Still, Teensy hadn't figured Gardner would lose his senses.

He'd let Gardner stew in his juices. Teensy was tired of being bullied by him—especially now. He wished the heifers good night and continued to walk toward the hill to where he'd parked hours ago. As he neared his truck, Teensy heard a click and spun around. He saw Gardner a few feet from the porch, balancing his rifle across the bars of the walker. "What the hell are you doing?" Teensy yelled, shining the flashlight in Gardner's direction. He stormed over to him.

"I might be feeble in body, but I ain't in mind. I know what you're doing, and I'm not going to allow it. Not while I'm still alive. You have them bring the most palsied group of heifers just to waste my hard-earned money."

"Your what?"

"You know it's true. What else you want me to do? Can't bring her back from the dead." Gardner's words were like stones plummeting into a gulley from a great distance.

Teensy made his voice calm. Pronounced each syllable with care. "Listen, I want this to be a success as well. Give it until morning." Teensy could feel the rifle between them, the long, smooth metal barrel. "I'll call the vet then," Teensy said. "We'll see what he has to say. I got as much riding on this as you," he added. And then neither one of them said anything. The light from the flashlight seemed faint in comparison to the stars and the glow from the barn fixture. From where he stood, he could still see the downed heifer. Teensy watched her grind her teeth, while all the other animals gave her a wide berth. He wanted to tell Gardner that he'd had cattle with shipping fever before and that a little rest righted them almost immediately. He wanted to say that now that they were here and these heifers were under his control, he wasn't going to fail them. The heifer readied her two front legs, gave a long cry, and appeared unable to rise.

"You should let her go now," Gardner said. "You let that kind of weakness in your herd, and you're only inviting trouble." He ran a hand along the barrel.

Teensy shook his head, but Gardner could not see this in the dark. "It'll be different come morning," he said, more sure now than ever. "You go on, head to bed. We'll deal with this tomorrow."

Gardner looked at him. "I think it's a mistake," he said, and his voice sounded like it pained him to speak.

"Objection noted." Darkness had come fast. Teensy thought of heading back toward his truck, where he knew he'd find a blanket and a warmer jacket and the dull bronze urn. But he remained in place.

Gardner hobbled with the rifle balanced across the frame of the walker. The gun slid across the metal, thudded to the ground. Teensy leaned over and picked up the rifle. He hefted its weight in his hands and thought of Luann falling through the trees from that great height, with Gardner at her side in the cab of the truck. One time Gardner had been in the haze of pain meds and Teensy had come in and heard him calling Luann's name.

"Chilly," Gardner said.

"Yes it is," Teensy said, pausing. He could feel Gardner watching him, felt the rush of the river's current as it pushed against the sinking truck, Gardner scrambling to get Luann out. Teensy took the rifle in one hand and held open the door to the house. He wanted to take Gardner's elbow and tell him he forgave him, tell him it would all be okay, but he held back. He knew the time wasn't quite right yet took his place beside him all the same.

FIRST BODY,
THEN MIND

THE CRY WOKE HIM. Teensy pushed up on his elbows from his place on the couch, squinted into the dark. Thought it might be Gardner. His legs no longer worked, and once a day a girl in a powder blue vest gave him the morphine. After last night's dose, Gardner lay down on his bed and gazed at the ceiling. White bits burrowed in his mouth corners. Teensy, exhausted from working the cattle, fell asleep on the couch.

Now Gardner snored strong in the other room, while outside the cries surged, gave Teensy that not-right twinge. He put on a coat, stepped into his boots, and went out. He figured one of the cows had probably ended up in the ravine. The shrubs were still empty of greenery, but the briar patch could trap a calf or two.

His boots broke through crusted ground with a satisfactory thunk. The moon shone full, but the bulb outside the barn, what should have burned bright, was dead.

By touch Teensy found the flashlight and shed the beam inside the barn. He found it empty save for three bawling calves, the gate on the other side flung wide. Teensy stepped outside the barn, raised the light, and now he saw that the fixture was busted. On the ground glass smattered with gravel. Goofballs, he thought. Some kids getting their kicks, screwing around.

There was another string of moans. Teensy hiked toward the ravine, and the bawling sounds gathered strength. The wind picked up and pushed at him from both sides. Teensy held the flashlight in front of him. The ground sloped, and he steadied himself on young trees. A thorny branch swatted his cheek and back of his hand. He sucked at the wound.

Cattle were curious creatures. They were always searching for their favorites—timothy and clover—even though Gardner's land, where Teensy was raising the beef cattle, offered some of the tastiest pasture in Ingleside.

The beam jostled as he moved, the moaning louder. He spotted a flash of black rump, a flank, and then the whole lot of them together at the foot of the ravine. What sort of mischief have you gotten yourselves into? he asked. A mama bellowed, danced an agitated two-step. I see you, he said. He put a hand out to pat her backside and calm her, but at his touch she cried fierce. He pulled back at the smell of blood. Some motion in his periphery made him turn around and aim the light up. He saw one of the calves hanging from the trees. It had been skinned, its hide dangling from its back legs, marbled flesh glistening as it creaked in the wind. His breath sucked away at the shock of it, its solid form swinging overhead. Teensy shone the light on the ground, brought a hand to his own neck, and petted the busted skin as if the gesture might halt the present. Wind whistled through the bare limbs. He swung the beam back.

Teensy saw where wire had been wrapped around the calves' front hooves and fixed in the branches. Its throat had been slit, and the meat wouldn't even be proper for butchering. Teensy breathed. Such waste. I'll get her down, he told them. Come on now, and he swatted their backsides. Git. He should have been surprised, but no amount of wrongdoing shocked him anymore.

Gardner had made himself a millionaire selling to the developers who bulldozed the trees to erect coasters. But now the park was empty of food stands and lacquered cars, the blacktop cracked and spotted with weeds. Gardner was dying—he was just a shadow of who he had used to be. Still, that wasn't enough for some people and their hatred. Now you couldn't make a living farming, and you couldn't make a living working in the park. Folks were not happy. Teensy considered calling the sheriff, but the idea left soon after it arrived. He wasn't ready to withstand their looks—what were two old men, one on his deathbed, doing raising cattle?

He wiped his mouth and started up the incline he'd just descended. He would need cutters and the ladder. Didn't want Gardner to know about the murdered calf. Arbuckle's son was supposed to come late morning and give him a hand. Teensy would do the work now and bury it. He heard quick footsteps on the gravel drive, the sound of the door to Gardner's house being opened far above and then slammed shut. Lock drawn.

Teensy stopped momentarily. Trained his ear and then picked up the pace. Had Gardner gotten himself in the wheelchair and pushed himself over to the door? He saw the outline of the house as he came out of the trees. It was as dark as he'd left it. He took the three steps up onto the porch and then rattled the door handle, metal solid and unmoving. *Gardner? You awake?* he called. *I'm out here. Lemme in.* Was the old coot trying to spook him or freeze him through?

Teensy banged his fist. He stood up in his boots and peered in the fine glass that spread across the top third of the door. The hall that led to Gardner's room was illuminated, but the door to his room remained closed. Teensy heard yelling and slamming drawers—voices that didn't belong to Gardner. Indistinct words. And then he jumped back from the door as if it had burned him. He felt blood drain from his hands and face. Someone other than Gardner was inside the house. Everything became spotty, and he had to put a hand on the doorframe to stay upright. He told himself to breathe. Breathe, goddamnit, and then, scared, he ducked behind a bush.

Teensy's heart thumped at an unnatural speed as he crouched just off the living room. He listened as things were turned over inside the house, smashed on the ground. The money's in the safe. It's upstairs, he thought. His stomach whirled, and he felt the bile rise. Don't get sick, he willed himself, not yet.

He fixed his eyes on Gardner's room. The light at the bottom of the door flashed as figures moved behind it. Teensy thought about Gardner. The man couldn't even swallow a bite of grilled cheese and had to drink his meals from a tiny plastic straw. After the girl restocked the tiny suitcase of pills, she gave him a sponge bath. Gardner couldn't even be trusted alone in the shower.

On a good day, when the headache had yet to descend and Gardner hadn't slipped into the morphine haze, he would talk about the pain. He had once explained to Teensy that in the white-hot heat of it, he could see the tumor's outline, feel its stretch in his head. His hands trembled all the time, and he held himself in the chair with the skittishness of a mouse. Not much longer now, Gardner would say. First the body, then the mind.

Gardner had probably wet his pants by now. Teensy wouldn't blame him if he did. In fact, he made a promise to clean Gardner himself. Teensy didn't want the girl to see Gardner like that. It'll be over soon, Teensy told himself. They both just needed to keep their wits.

Gardner said something, and a voice erupted, Shut up, old man!

Teensy stood there, his fingers froze through. And he again felt a flurry of nausea. He made himself turn away from the window and face the sky, with its black uncertainty and endless parade of stars. He breathed in the smell of the river, the dormant grasses and metallic scent of fertilizer from long ago. It was the smell of Ingleside. As familiar as the reflection of his own face in a mirror.

Whoever these punks were, they were likely there to rough up the old man, take his wallet and that fancy watch of his. Teensy squatted beneath the window. But then he heard crying—real pleading from Gardner—and he plugged his ears.

He should go for help. Even if it took an hour of his fastest walking, he knew he should do it—but his feet stayed still.

This your revenge? asked a hollow voice from his gut. No. He shook his head. He'd forgiven Gardner. It had been years now, and the man couldn't even stand up long enough to relieve himself. He thought of Luann, of the empty urn standing on his mantle. What Gardner had done to Luann had been an accident. Teensy wasn't interested in staking claim on the man's soul. Seeing Gardner moving around in that chair, all the parts that didn't work anymore, forced to expose himself to that little girl in the blue vest. Teensy didn't want any part of it.

The bedroom door flung open, and Teensy saw them. Black knit caps on their heads and the still doughy jaws of youth. He watched them bound up the stairs like a couple of kids on Christmas. The fixtures came on in the hallway on the second floor. Maybe Gardner had given them the key after all. It was the land that mattered. The cattle, frightened as they might be, were already here.

From his place near the window, Teensy watched the front door. Figured if he could break it down, he could probably carry Gardner outside, gaunt as he was. But then the punks might hear him, and he doubted they planned on seeing Teensy. A brisk wind threaded the branches. As soon as these idiots got their money, they'd scram. Gardner just needed to hang tight.

The moon hung low, the gleam of it almost reverberating. Teensy wondered how he'd fallen asleep the night before in the first place. He heard thumping upstairs, drawers being opened and turned over. Just making one giant mess. Teensy and the girl would be charged with the cleanup. He spied a truck out on the road. He craned his neck, tried to see the plates. Even if he did call the sheriff, he wouldn't be able to do much. The town didn't have funds to hold anyone more than a few days.

Teensy breathed into his hands. Heat seeped out his fingers. There were lots of folks who felt bitter toward Gardner, toward what he'd done, selling land, having money. Maybe it served him right to be shaken up. Let him see how rough other people had it. Lord knew there were weeks Teensy had nothing but peanut butter and saltines in his belly, a Tupperware of Kool-Aid in the refrigerator. When had Gardner ever missed a meal, sweat seeping his shirt because he had enough for the mortgage but not the electric bill?

Papers fluttered down the stairs. Heavy things pushed over. If Gardner had told them the safe was upstairs and given them the key, what was taking so long?

The cattle filled Teensy's ears with their lowing. In his mind he saw the skinned calf rocking in the branches, body twisting numb. He didn't know what kind of lowlife could harm an innocent like that. Out of the corner of his eye he noticed the bedroom door creep open, the light going wide. Teensy saw that it was Gardner's hand on the doorjamb, only he wasn't in the chair. He dragged himself across the floor, a palsied half-crawl. Gardner's mouth, what he could see of it, was swollen on one side. His jaw purpled and his eyes looked lopsided, like someone had shaken the old man and things had yet to settle back into place. He looked to be moving into the living room then thought better of it, craned his neck and turned back around toward the bedroom. He slipped along in the trousers and T-shirt he'd worn the previous day. When the girl came, she'd give him his bath, dress him in clean clothes. Gardner looked withered and thinner than ever, but Teensy gladdened at the sight of him. He raised a hand. Hey! he said, inside his head, I'm right out here.

After she cleaned him up, the girl would pop the can on one of those nutrition drinks. Gardner liked vanilla best, although he smacked his mouth afterward, made a weird face. You know it's bad when you can't even eat a burger no more, he had said.

Teensy watched Gardner slither across the floor and then pull himself onto his knees, legs folded behind him. Teensy tapped a fingernail on the window and then waved. They were creating a racket upstairs, and it was too loud to hear much of anything. Teensy could only see the bottom part of Gardner's legs, but from that angle he could tell he was rooting around in the closet, searching for something. Then he sat ramrod straight against the wall, his back to Teensy.

Later Teensy would go to the liquor store and get Gardner whatever he wanted—one of the meds made him sick when he took a drink, and Teensy would make the girl tell him which one did this, and then he'd go to the row of pills near the kitchen sink and toss the whole bottle in the trash.

From where he stood, Teensy could see Gardner's profile, the jagged chip of his chin and the tuft of white hair that flopped over his forehead. Then he righted himself and turned his head, and only part of it showed. His hands were hidden behind the wall, but Teensy could tell by the movement of his arms that he was fiddling with something. He tipped his chin up to one side, and Teensy thought his friend had finally heard him. I'm right here. I've been here the whole time, he'd later tell him over drinks or a plate of eggs over easy—whatever soft food Gardner wanted, Teensy would fix.

Teensy was waving wildly at Gardner when the shot went off.

Gardner's head flung back, his body jerked to the rear, and the rest of him went limp. He slumped into the open doorway. Teensy's breath left him, and he felt himself break up, dissolve. He fingered his chest, could only make out the sound of his own heart beating. He bent over and vomited in the bushes.

The men came running, took steps two at a time, and when they got to the bedroom said, What the fuck? Oh man, oh man! Blood splattered the door, pooled the floor, Gardner's upper half twisted sideways.

Here was Teensy's chance to rush in, jump them. If he hurried, he could get an ambulance to take Gardner to the hospital. He thought these things rapid fire while his body remained mute. Years ago he worked at a beef processing plant a few months before he got on again at Papermill, and he remembered the hulking bodies of cattle heaped at his feet.

Adrenaline fueled him, and Teensy rushed the door. He kicked at it, but it remained solid. He was going for another strike when the door flung open and he fell forward on the floor. Teensy absorbed the warmth of the house. Who are you? one of them asked, but the other was already on him in the darkness with one of Gardner's pistols.

He lifted his hands. He wanted to ask what they wanted, why they were here. But he heard the crack of bones and felt a massive jolt on the side of his head. His teeth felt loose in their sockets.

Let's go, said the one.

Asshole, said the other and spit, the warm ball sliding down Teensy's cheek; he followed this with a kick. Teensy covered his head with his arms.

All the lights in the house were off save for Gardner's bedroom, and from where Teensy sprawled flattened on the floor, the room seemed to glow. The drawers were overturned, the mattress slashed, foam exposed like innards. There was a faint odor of urine. He waited for the flashing lights, approaching sirens. He was alive, he told himself. Just sit tight. His hand throbbed. Don't think, breathe. He was safe. Outside in the darkness he heard the bald cry of the mama cow. A lump held in his throat that he could not swallow away. He was not proud of the chilled feeling that crept along his skin. He blamed it on the pain that pulsed from his head, this odd sense that Gardner had gotten what he deserved. They just wanted to shake you, he thought, and then recalled the sound of the gun going off. He knew the old man was dead.

Gardner's yellow-oiled smell penetrated the air. I did all I could, Teensy told himself as he crafted a story for the sheriff, the newspapers. How he'd burst in and tried to save Gardner during the robbery. Teensy thought of Gardner in his wheelchair, his parts unworking. Everything below Teensy's waist buzzed limp. He lifted his head, planted the busted hand on the floor, and tried to pull himself forward, to slide along like Gardner had done. If only he was strong enough.

CHAINS

THE HEIFER IS DOWN AND HAVING CONTRACTIONS every few minutes, her abdomen quaking, but two hours in, and her mouth has already gone foamy, with no part of the calf exposed. I put the sleeves on again to check. I can only go in as far as my forearms when I feel the bony protrusion of the calf's nose, the tip of her front feet. Good job, mama, I tell her, although I'm worried. Her water ruptured two hours ago, and by now she should be nursing the calf, and I should be snug in bed. The calf's gonna be more than eighty pounds, maybe closer to ninety, and she's a first-time heifer with a small pelvis.

I sip coffee from a thermos and screw the cap tight. The sound of peepers fills the air, the night balmy and sweet. It's gonna be okay, I tell her. Between contractions she cranes her neck and looks up at me, and the overhead bulb pins her eyes with white globes. Her nostrils split wide as she pants; she struggles inside the cage of each contraction, and with the jerky rise of her stomach, I realize that I'm going to lose her.

I could try for the vet, but the phone is in the house, and I know enough that by the time he gets out here and shoots me a stern look, it will be too late. I should have called him hours ago. Now I don't have any choice but to use the chains.

The heifer stretches her neck to sit upright but has forgotten about the calf and all the weight that keeps her back end moored. Unable to rise, she sticks out her tongue, tries to reach a bunch of hay. She stops calving and chews, looks off in the direction of the barn opening. She wants to go out with the rest of them, their moos reaching up into the night sky as free and natural as anything. Her pink tongue rolls out toward the hay, and I think that this was what it was for her mother and great-grandmother and every cow in her lineage; for hundreds of years before now, the fight against the body and the calf that would not come ended under the sugar maples and sycamores, alongside rows of corn just beginning to spear the earth. The cows before this good heifer would just go down, sweat bees and blackflies wheeling, an unnecessary human far off somewhere; her heavy head would list to the side, the massive pen of her belly growing still. I feel the urge coming off her. Feel her pull toward something beyond.

I'll have none of it. Not yet. I restrain her in a halter, tie the tail up and to the side, then rewash my hands and scrub her back end with soap, rinsing the area with fresh water and patting her dry with paper towels. I get the chains and soap them good. I try to think about the times I've seen the vet use them—go over the steps in my mind fully aware that I could kill the heifer or calf or both. I try and remember to breathe.

I put on fresh gloves and push firm to get inside the heifer's rear, then loop each chain around the front legs and above the hooves. I pull on one leg, then the other—just a few inches at a time. I imagine all the cattle that once pounded this earth whispering her name from the unplanted fields, calling her home with some secret animal plea. I'm not giving her to you, I say. She's staying right here.

The heifer tries to turn, to see what's unfolding, but the halter holds her steady. She's awake, moos constant. I pull harder, and nothing happens. I let go and slip out of the heifer. She moos, the chains are hanging out of her, and I can't do it. I don't know what I'm doing.

I leave the area of the barn I've cleaned and step out to gulp air. The sky has brightened, and a kind breeze rustles the leaves. The smell of the river rises up—its earthy decay rich even from a mile away—and I know it's Luann, telling me to try again, not to give up. Words she never spoke in life come freely now. Okay, I think. Once more.

I put on fresh gloves and go back in, work the chains a bit gentler. The left shoulder appears, and I rotate the calf a quarter-turn, provide traction to the front legs, and pull toward the heifer's side. We are making progress. One hipbone goes through and then the other, and the calf slides out in a steamy wet black blob. My heart hums full and bright—I did it, we did it, I think. I clear mucus from the calf's mouth and throat. She starts breathing. I undo the head catch, and the heifer begins to lick the calf.

When I stand, I feel my body for the first time in hours. There's a calmness in me that feels right and good. I make my hands fists—one, then the other—just because I can. I step outside the barn. The sky has shifted from purple to pinky orange. I'm going to call the vet to make up for last night's foolishness, then make myself a steak and fried potatoes. I can almost smell the coffee.

The grass is wet, and brown-skinned weeds are flat from where they've trod. The day's heat comes later now, the sun gathering strength in the early afternoon. I'm thinking about food and my bed, but the day is going to be a long one, and who am I kidding? There is no time for sleep. I start toward the house, moving thick as butter, when the dog starts barking that rapid *yap yap yap*. Too early for the mail, I think, and then my feet become cement blocks. Morning just breaking, and I see a youthful form. Can't be the vet. Haven't given word to anyone about the heifer or her delivery. I head toward the shape that comes down the slope from the house, all that light rising up behind him. Just when you think the day's going to be one way, it turns and takes you somewhere else altogether, and that place is so miraculous and full of wonder that if you'd spent your lifetime dreaming, you still would not have imagined this.

I was alone at the coroner when the news of Luann's death finally sunk in, not a window in sight. A dusty artificial plant prevailed as witness. The end of her life, you see, began the second half of mine.

The young man walking toward me has a jelly-armed loose-ness. My eyes go soft, fingers numb at the familiarity of her gate and how it's been reincarnated. I don't understand. Not right away. Maybe it's all a dream. I've been awake a long time. I rub my eyes to clear them. If it's a dream, it's a cruel one—Luann brought back as a boy. But it's not a joke. He's here—rather, she's here—those curls, scooped forehead, and olive skin. I'd recognize him anywhere. We stare for a long moment before he says it, and when he does, it's like he's already spoken the words. I'm looking for Luann Teensy, he says, and I nod. I start shaking and can't breathe. I am old. What's to say what is real, what is imagined? The sun glints on the drain spout in the distance. I have to lean over to catch my breath, hang onto my knees; afraid I'll drop over, but I don't want to turn my eyes from him, so I kind of squint at his face—he looks just like her as a youngster—shrouded in sun. You okay? he asks, voice still settling into its adolescent self. The night has been so long, and I am tired. He reaches out a hand, and I take it, rise.

To order or obtain more information on these or other
University of Nebraska Press titles, visit nebraskapress.unl.edu.

CPSIA information can be obtained
at www.ICGtesting.com
Printed in the USA
LVOW08s2042300817
546976LV00002B/252/P